D1598452

The Graveside Bar and Grill

Also From Darynda Jones

YOUNG ADULT

DARKLIGHT SERIES
Death and the Girl Next Door
Death, Doom, and Detention
Death and the Girl He Loves

The Graveside Bar and Grill
A Charley Davidson Novella
By Darynda Jones

1001 DARK NIGHTS

PRESS

The Graveside Bar and Grill
A Charley Davidson Novella
By Darynda Jones

1001 Dark Nights

Copyright 2022 Darynda Jones
ISBN: 979-8-88542-003-7

Foreword: Copyright 2014 M. J. Rose

Published by 1001 Dark Nights Press, an imprint of Evil Eye Concepts,
Incorporated

Acknowledgments from the Author

Thank you soooo much, Grimlets, for being as excited about this story as I was to write it! I missed Donovan and the gang, so this was a super fun project.

Thank you, as always, to my incredible agent, Alexandra Machinist, without whom the Charley world would not exist to such a spectacular degree. And to my amazing film agent, Josie Freedman. I love working with you both.

Thank you to Lorelei King for bringing all things Charley to life. It's been over a decade! Where would Charley be without your sexy-ass voice mesmerizing her readers?

And most especially thank you to Liz, Jillian, and MJ for putting up with me and being there through every step of this story. I'm so very honored to work with you.

And then there's Chelle. I can't even. You amaze me. I appreciate your talent more than you can know.

Thank you to my wonderful, amazing assistants, Netters, Dana, and Trayce.

Thank you to the lurves of my life, my family, who let me hug and kiss on them in public with very few complaints.

And again, Grimlets! You inspire me to do my very best. Thank you for sticking with Charley and the gang through thick and thin. Mostly thick. Lots of thick.

One Thousand and One Dark Nights

Once upon a time, in the future…

*I was a student fascinated with stories and learning.
I studied philosophy, poetry, history, the occult, and
the art and science of love and magic. I had a vast
library at my father's home and collected thousands
of volumes of fantastic tales.*

*I learned all about ancient races and bygone
times. About myths and legends and dreams of all
people through the millennium. And the more I read
the stronger my imagination grew until I discovered
that I was able to travel into the stories... to actually
become part of them.*

*I wish I could say that I listened to my teacher
and respected my gift, as I ought to have. If I had, I
would not be telling you this tale now.
But I was foolhardy and confused, showing off
with bravery.*

*One afternoon, curious about the myth of the
Arabian Nights, I traveled back to ancient Persia to
see for myself if it was true that every day Shahryar
(Persian: شهریار, "king") married a new virgin, and then
sent yesterday's wife to be beheaded. It was written
and I had read that by the time he met Scheherazade,
the vizier's daughter, he'd killed one thousand
women.*

*Something went wrong with my efforts. I arrived
in the midst of the story and somehow exchanged
places with Scheherazade — a phenomena that had
never occurred before and that still to this day, I
cannot explain.*

*Now I am trapped in that ancient past. I have
taken on Scheherazade's life and the only way I can
protect myself and stay alive is to do what she did to
protect herself and stay alive.*

*Every night the King calls for me and listens as I spin tales.
And when the evening ends and dawn breaks, I stop at a
point that leaves him breathless and yearning for more.
And so the King spares my life for one more day, so that
he might hear the rest of my dark tale.*

*As soon as I finish a story... I begin a new
one... like the one that you, dear reader, have before
you now.*

Chapter One

Sorry I'm late.
I didn't want to come.
—T-shirt often seen on Charley Davidson

When the teenage daughter of two gods asks you to keep an eye on the beautiful doctor who takes care of her merry band of misfits—no questions asked—that is exactly what you do.

Not that Donovan St. James was whipped. He wasn't. He'd never been whipped a day in his life. At least, not until the two most important people in his life came into the world. First, his son. A ten-year-old with more swagger than he had any right to. And then again when Elwyn Alexandra Loehr, screaming velociraptor that she was, decided to grace humanity with her presence. Before either of those entries, he never would have believed that something so tiny could render him powerless with a single glance.

But Teacup ordering him around like he was somehow in her servitude was too much. If not for the fact that said doctor—a gorgeous redhead with curves that screamed *slippery when wet*—walked into his bar minutes after he received the odd request, he would've texted the teacup back a hard *no*. He wouldn't have sent it, but he would've typed it into his phone—probably in all caps—and smirked in satisfaction before deleting it and texting instead: *When you say no questions asked...*

I'm just worried about her, Elwyn messaged back. *She seems distraught.*

Distraught? Donovan huffed out a laugh from behind the bar and shook his head. What the hell kind of kid used the word *distraught?*

Distraught in what way? Brainiac.

She shot him an eye-roll emoji, then sent: *You have to stop calling me that. I'm not a brainiac. I'm just well-traveled.*

That was the understatement of the century. The kid had recently slipped onto another plane and then got lost there. While her journey had only lasted three days here on Earth, she'd been gone for years on the planes she'd traveled while trying to find her way back home. It was a tragedy Donovan had yet to come to terms with. She'd left a sassy, precocious, coffee-drinking five-year-old and returned a bossy teen with a god complex.

It broke his heart that he'd missed most of her childhood. They all had. And he questioned for the thousandth time why he stayed. Why he subjected himself to such strife and anguish. She had suffered. He saw it in the aging of her eyes. The sadness behind her smile. If he hadn't sworn on his life that he would protect the girl destined to save humanity, he would've put Santa Fe, New Mexico in his rearview ages ago. But that promise, along with the fact that he loved the elfin more than the life he'd sworn on kept him glued to the area, no matter the turmoil. Or the apprehension.

But no one had told him he'd be taking orders from the little tyrant. He snorted aloud at her *well-traveled* comment, drawing the attention of his fill-in bartender, a last-minute replacement with long, chestnut hair, shimmering golden eyes, and a T-shirt that read: *May my morning coffee give me the strength to make my mid-morning coffee.* She was also a god and the mother of said tyrant.

Charley Davidson sashayed over to him and gave him a saucy wink. A saucy wink that Donovan ignored since her husband—a god, as well, as luck would have it—was sitting three stools away from him. Thankfully, a bar took up space between them. A bulwark, so to speak. A barrier that could give him a split-second advantage should he need it.

Not that he would, but it was nice to have options.

He turned and watched as the redhead wound her way through the sparse patronage to a corner booth. She slipped into it, the shadows sliding over her until they almost completely consumed her. He made a mental note to up the wattage on the lamp hanging over that particular table. All he could make out now was a shapely calf that spilled down into a red, low-heeled pump.

Charley broke into the seedier side of his thoughts that arose at the sight of the red pump by sidling up to him. She propped an elbow on his shoulder and said, "I like her."

Donovan nodded, trying to make out the rest of the doctor's outline. "Me, too." Then he turned toward the radiant woman leaning lazily against him and realized that she was looking in the opposite direction. He refocused on the end of the bar. "You like who?"

Charley pointed to her husband, who sat with a woman on either side of him, each doing her best to flirt. *Good luck with that.*

"You like the women flirting with the man you vowed to love for all eternity?" And in this couple's case, that was a real possibility. An eternity seemed like such a long time to be shackled to one person. But after being alone for so long, he'd take it.

"No," she said with a snort. "I only like the one on his left. The raven-haired beauty with the Brazilian accent. She gives good aura."

He squinted at the two women he'd noticed the moment they walked in—as had everyone at the bar. The dark-haired one wore a rust-colored T-shirt and a cowgirl hat, clearly trying to blend with the locals. The blonde wore a shimmering powder-blue cocktail dress, which was a little too fancy for his establishment, a biker den called The Graveside Bar and Grill. Apropos since it sat next to a cemetery.

"But you don't like the flashy blonde who speaks fluent socialite?"

"Nope," Charley said. "She's about as batshit as batshit comes."

"Ah. So you *do* still have it."

She leveled those sparkling eyes on him, looking askance. "Have what?"

"*It.*" He gestured toward her with the towel he'd been using to dry glasses. "You know, that thing where you can read people's minds."

She crinkled one corner of her mouth. "I can't read minds, boss."

Every time she filled in at the bar, she called him *boss.* He couldn't help but shake his head at the irony of it. She and her husband were rich-as-fuck gods as old as time itself. For real. He couldn't make that shit up if he tried—he'd never been that creative.

"I can only read emotions," she continued, her admonishing tone making it sound like he was a stone's throw away from becoming the village idiot. "Of the living, anyway. And right now, she's only pretending to be into Dr. Farrow."

"Dr. Farrow?" He turned back to the trio. "When exactly did your husband have time to go to medical school?" Especially since the two of them had spent the last five years in celestial bliss, watching over their daughter from the heavens. They'd only recently decided to come back to Earth after the girl's recent jaunt abroad—to be closer to their daughter should she need them.

But that was the part he didn't understand. Charley Davidson and Reyes Farrow—aka, the grim reaper and the son of Satan—had come back incognito, so to speak. Elwyn had no clue that the owners of her new favorite coffee shop were her biological parents. But why? *Why* keep their identities a secret?

Though he had yet to get around to it, Donovan vowed to get to the bottom of their subterfuge. He knew they had their reasons. And they were likely damned good ones if he knew Charley Davidson. He just wanted to know what they were.

"I have no idea," Charley said, answering his question. "But that man is a prodigy when it comes to female anatomy. Medical school is the only explanation." She looked up in thought and pursed her lips, causing dimples to form on either side of her mouth. "Although I suppose there could be one other explanation." She bounced back and refocused on her dark husband. A husband whose eyes were locked on her, despite the companion he had on either arm. "Nope. That's the only possible explanation."

A hint of a smile flashed across Farrow's face as though he could hear every word his wife said. The place wasn't exactly hopping, but it was loud enough to make hearing a quiet conversation from ten feet away difficult. Especially with *Sweet Home Alabama* cranked up and coming through the speakers. Even so, the fact that Farrow could hear their conversation hardly surprised Donovan. The man was a celestial being, after all.

Charley crossed her arms over her chest and studied her man.

He studied her back.

"I am clearly not using my husband to his full potential." Charley refocused on Donovan. "Can he make a mean mocha latte?"

"No idea."

"Yes. Can he whip up a batch of chocolate syrup I'd pay to bathe in?"

"Let me guess..."

"Yes. But is that enough?"

Though the question was clearly rhetorical, he answered, "I'm guessing no."

"Exactly." She pointed her chin at the errant man. "We could make a fortune using his medical degree to become an OBGYN to the stars. Rich women love sexy doctors."

Donovan cleared his throat and went back to drying glasses. "TMI. But thanks, sweetheart. And why is she only pretending?"

Charley blinked at him. "Who?"

"The blonde." Donovan gestured toward the woman. "You said she's only *pretending* to be into your lesser half."

"Oh, right." Charley eased closer and lowered her voice. "Think about it. You're here with a stunning Brazilian and only pretending to be into the hot guy at the bar. Why do you think she'd do that?" When he only raised a brow, she rolled her eyes, looking so much like her daughter it stunned him for a minute. "To spend more time with her crush."

"The Brazilian," he said matter-of-factly.

"Now, you're getting it."

"So, she's in love with her friend. *Why* does that make her batshit?"

"Because the jealousy pulsing out of her is bright and sharp. It's like staring into one of those huge lamps in a lighthouse without blinking. I'm a little worried for the Brazilian." She wiped down the bar, making her way closer to Farrow.

Her husband winked at her, again obviously in on their conversation, then looked at Donovan as he joined them. "I need a dime," he said.

Charley tsked. "I gave you a dollar before we left the house. Did you spend it all already?"

When Farrow only grinned at her and leveled a purposeful stare on Donovan, he frowned and reached into his pocket. Not without complaint, however. "Why do you need a dime? I thought you were a billionaire."

His comment surprised both women. The Brazilian raised a brow, impressed, but the blonde seemed to take a more active interest in the man beside her. She slunk closer and slipped an arm into his.

"Not that kind of dime," Farrow said when Donovan tossed a coin onto the counter.

"Ah." Donovan reached under the bar and pulled out a white, dime-shaped disc. He handed the paper object over and waited.

Farrow set it on the bar as both women looked on curiously. Then he turned the full power of his charm—if one could call it that—on the Brazilian by locking gazes with her.

The woman flashed him a nuclear smile that stayed in place even when he dipped a finger into her margarita. As though more curious than surprised, she looked down and watched as he tapped his wet finger on the disc, depositing two thick droplets onto it. The paper absorbed them immediately.

That was when Donovan noticed the blonde's smile. It faltered just a little, and tension slid across her shoulders slightly as she straightened unconsciously. She tightened her cheeks, forcing her expression to hold steady, unable to take her eyes off the disc.

Slowly, one pink line emerged.

The Brazilian's pretty brows slid together. "What does that mean?" she asked, her thick accent somehow cute and sexy at the same time.

"It means," Donovan said, taking both the disc and margarita and putting them behind the bar, "that someone slipped a narcotic into your drink."

Her jaw dropped slightly as she studied Farrow, seeming even more confused than before.

Donovan knew what she was thinking. Why would a man at a bar drug her and then test the drink for drugs? She had yet to notice that her companion's face had paled, and her friend clutched her bag to her chest. At least Donovan now knew where to find her stash.

"Rohypnol is such a nasty way to get a date," Donovan said to the blonde. He snapped his fingers at his bouncer, a biker with shady ties to the mafia.

Michael walked over to them as though annoyed at being summoned. It was a mafioso thing. Donovan could give his best friend a hundred-dollar tip, and the man would act as though it were beneath him to take it. But take it he would.

Clearly stunned, the Brazilian leaned back, looking at her friend from around Farrow.

Donovan gestured toward the blonde as he spoke to Michael. "Would you help this young lady to my office and call the police?"

"Will do." Michael nodded at the blonde, who abruptly stood as though readying to run. "I wouldn't," he said to her. "It'll only piss me off."

She clamped her jaw shut and glared at the lot of them. "You can't keep me here."

"Actually, we can," he said as he slid a large hand around her arm.

"I'm calling my lawyer," she said.

Michael escorted her toward the back. "You're going to need one."

"Did she...?" The Brazilian was clearly still wrapping her head around what'd just happened. Her gaze flitted from Donovan to Charley and then back to Farrow. "Why would she try to drug me?"

Charley answered for them. "I suspect she was worried you'd try to go home with my husband."

The Brazilian's shocked gaze landed on Farrow again. "You're married?" When he only nodded, the disappointment that flashed across her face was impossible to miss.

"I completely understand," Charley said. "Would you like another less-chemically-enhanced margarita?"

The woman sank onto her stool. "No. I think I'm done drinking for a while."

Charley nodded and poured her some sparkling water instead. She set it on the bar in front of her and then asked, "Are you rich? Because I'm thinking about putting him on the market." She tipped her chin at her husband. "I need a little spending money."

"Oh, no," the dark-haired woman said, seeming a thousand miles away. She absently waved a hand and then snapped her attention back to them when Charley's meaning finally sank in. She looked Farrow up and down, then added, "But if I were, I'd pay top dollar."

A devastating smile widened across Charley's face, and Donovan pretended not to be affected by it. "That's so sweet," she said, covering the woman's hand with hers for a quick squeeze. She was so good with people. So caring. *Too* caring, according to her husband.

Farrow took a sip of his drink and then broke into Donovan's thoughts by asking, "Have you been flirting with my wife again?"

"Again?" Donovan asked, deciding to wipe down the bar. "I never stopped. How'd you know?"

"I have eyes," Farrow answered.

Charley snorted.

"No," Donovan said. "I mean how'd you know about the drink? Did you use your superpowers or something?"

Farrow frowned, seemingly unimpressed. "Superpowers?"

"You have money *and* superpowers?" the Brazilian asked.

"He does," Charley said to her before leaning closer to her husband. "And, of course, Donovan still flirts with me. Have you seen my ass?" She gave Farrow a wink before sauntering off to see to the customers on the other side of the bar.

Farrow took a long, hard look at that very ass before pointing to the mirror behind the bar. "I saw her pour something from a small vial into your drink. It'll still be in her bag."

"Oh, my God. I can't imagine why she would do that. We've been friends for almost two years. Why throw that away?"

Why, indeed. Donovan left them to their conversation until the cops arrived. He made drinks for a table of tourists raving about *Meow Wolf*, at least according to his server, Eric—another biker who got bumped from bartender to server when Donovan's newest hire called in with the latest contagion. Thus his need to bring in his pinch hitter. Aka, Charley. Had he known she'd invite her husband...

Nah, he still would've called. Farrow was good for business. Once word got out that he was here, the place would fill up within an hour. The group of female patrons currently rushing inside his establishment, looks of feral excitement on their flushed faces, proved that. He'd have to invite the surly billionaire in more often.

One of the new customers ordered a drink for Farrow before she even sat down. Donovan filled the order and took it over to the man as two cops talked to him and the Brazilian, getting the story before they headed back to the office.

Charley walked up and propped an arm on Donovan's shoulder again. "Do you feel that?"

He turned to look at her, suddenly not sure he was in the mood to put up with an entire bar full of Farrow fans. "My burning desire to be born a rock in my next life?"

"No." She spun and looked at the door to the kitchen. It swung as if someone had just walked through it, but both of Donovan's servers were working the floor. "Like something is off." She dried her hands and took a step toward the kitchen before turning back to her husband. "Do you feel it?"

Though he was busy corroborating the Brazilian's story, Farrow nodded without looking over at them.

"See?" Charley said, as though that confirmed everything. "I haven't felt anything like that in a long time."

Having no clue what she was going on about, Donovan slid his gaze to the booth as he had every few seconds since the doc had arrived. A group of twenty-somethings sat there now. "Shit," he said when he realized his mark had slipped out when he wasn't looking. "She's gone."

Chapter Two

One word can change someone's
entire day: Margarita
—Meme

She should've known better. Actually, she *would've* known better had she not panicked. But she'd lost contact with the others, one by one. She could no longer hear their thoughts. So, when she discovered that Elle-Ryn-Ahleethia—or Charley Davidson as those on this plane knew her—would be tending bar at Donovan's establishment, she'd decided to take a chance. If anyone could help, it would be a god. A very powerful one from what Zhou remembered. No, not Zhou. *Sia.* Her name was Sia here. And then she'd seen her. Charley Davidson. The celestial being she hadn't set eyes on in five years. Whatever Sia had expected to find, it hadn't been... this. It wasn't a human where a god should have been.

And the man at the end of the bar with a woman on either arm, what was that about? Was he her husband? The god who'd been tricked by an entity called Satan to create a son? If that was the husband, Charley hadn't been kidding all those years ago. He *was* a gorgeous being. Not that he had anything on Donovan St. James, but to each their own.

At least she'd gotten to see Donovan again. That particular human had filled Sia's dreams with salacious fantasies since she landed on this rock five years ago. It must be the body she now inhabited. She'd found it on the brink of death in a dark alley and waited. Far be it from her to change the woman's history.

It hadn't taken long. At the exact moment Dr. Lucia Mirabal's soul left the woman's body, Zhou entered it to become the tenacious doctor known to her friends as Sia. Corporeal possession was all in the timing—and nine-tenths of the law.

When she inhabited it, all the doctor's knowledge had spilled into her, allowing Zhou to pick up where Dr. Lucia Mirabal had left off. After a lengthy hospital stay, that was. The body still had to recover from the wounds the attacker had inflicted.

But all the baggage that came with said body was proving more hindrance than help to Sia now. Humans had these annoying little parasites called hormones that seemed to control both the physical and the mental well-being to an alarming degree. And they were proving far more complicated than a simple *ka-zhouah*, one who'd spent centuries trapped in a dark void while slowly being drained of her energy, would've imagined. But seeing him again, possibly for the last time, was worth the risk of being found out. Of Charley recognizing her and, fearing for her daughter's safety from a sentient being with a questionable history, vanquishing her before she had a chance to explain.

Either way, Charley was human now. It mystified Sia how that was even possible. How did one go from being a god to a human? Maybe it was a trick of some kind. A mystical cloak to make other preternatural entities only *think* she was human. If it were, it'd worked. She'd fooled Sia, and Sia was never easily fooled.

One of Donovan's best friends was working as a bouncer tonight. A biker named Michael. She recognized both him and Donovan's other best friend, a younger kid named Eric, who looked like a movie star. After a commotion of some kind, Donovan summoned Michael over to the bar. A few seconds later, Michael escorted one of the women to the back. It all looked rather ominous—and became Sia's cue to leave.

She took one last look at the scruffy biker behind the bar. Or, more pointedly, at his wild, dark hair and impossibly broad shoulders.

"What can I get you, Doc?" Eric asked. He was playing server tonight, which was unusual. Everything about that night was strange, though Eric did look adorable with an apron tied around his waist.

She wondered if Donovan was wearing similar garb. He wore pants so well, surely an apron tied around his hips would look just as magnificent. In fact, she imagined that anything would look good wrapped around his hips—including her legs.

"Would you like some suggestions?" Eric prodded.

She snapped out of her thoughts and punished herself by digging her nails into her palms. She'd lost contact with the only family she'd known for the last twelve centuries and was now sitting in a bar drooling over the biker who'd stolen her heart.

"No, thanks. I'll just have—" The phone she'd set on the table dinged, and her gaze darted hopefully to the screen. It paid off. It was Benji. But why couldn't she hear his thoughts? It didn't matter where any of them were in the world, they could always communicate just as easily as they had in the void.

"I'm sorry," she said, sliding out of the booth and raising her phone in reference. "I have to take this."

"No, problem, Doc. I'll just get you a club soda for now."

"That's perfect. Thank you."

He flashed her a Hollywood smile as she stepped into an area she assumed led to the restrooms. Instead, she found herself in a small but industrial kitchen.

"Sorry," she said to the two employees who stopped what they were doing to look at her. Then she spotted another door that seemed to lead outside. That worked, too. "Sorry," she said again, hurrying past metal prep tables and a stainless-steel gas stove. She knew her presence in the kitchen was a code violation.

She opened the metal door and stumbled down two steps into a dark alley. A dumpster sat across from her, and several crates and boxes littered the area closest to her. After glancing around to make sure that no one was listening, she reread the text before trying to call Benji mentally. His text had simply asked: *Where are you?*

She pressed the call button on her cell and waited.

A staticky voice picked up. "Zhou?"

"Benji?" she half-whispered, half-hissed into the phone. "Where have you been? I can't hear you. I can't hear anyone. What's going on?"

"I don't know." His voice sounded garbled as if the signal was cutting in and out. He lived in an area with horrible service, but that'd never been an issue before. Not when they could carry on entire conversations in their minds. "I can't—"

Sia groaned when the connection dropped and tried calling back, to no avail. So, she texted. *What is going on?*

As she waited, she paced the uneven ground, looking over her shoulder every few seconds until her feet couldn't handle it anymore. Even in low heels, the balls of her feet were beginning to ache. She'd been on them all day, taking a turn at the clinic on 5th to keep her mind occupied. To stop it from racing with all the thoughts of what could've happened to the only family she'd ever known.

Five of them had made it out of the void on Charley Davidson's heels when she escaped, and they'd all found humans to inhabit soon after. Benji, as he was called on this plane, lived the closest to her. The others had had to search farther for acceptable candidates.

In order to inhabit a body at the time of its occupant's passing, it had to be in a particular condition. Its survival had to be plausible. Others needed to believe that the human could live, no matter what ordeal they'd suffered. The physical form had to be intact and able to thrive, despite the fact that, in reality, it hadn't. Having someone magically heal after being devoured by cancer for years was not a good option.

Zhou's candidate hadn't been in great condition when she'd found her, but the doctor could have certainly survived since she'd gotten medical attention relatively fast. And Zhou had liked that Sia was a doctor. She would be a respectable member of society and have a steady income.

On the other hand, Benji had stumbled upon a middle school student who'd fallen off a bridge into freezing water while roughhousing with his friends. The fall had actually killed the kid. The water was shallow, and he'd broken his neck on some rocks. But his survival could be explained, in that the cold had slowed his heart rate and allowed him to live for the forty-five minutes he'd been submerged in the water before his rescue. It'd taken a few weeks in the hospital to heal the broken neck, but his parents were overjoyed when he could walk and talk again.

Sia squelched the pang of jealousy that arose over the fact that Benji had found a host with a family—a loving family at that. It was something none of them had ever had. But why would he need to call her now? What was going on? Was there some kind of interference? If so, Sia wanted to know what the hell kind of signal jammer could block their ability to communicate telepathically. If it wasn't that, it would mean…

No. The alternative was too scary to even imagine. Besides, it had been five years. If he'd followed them from the void onto this plane, why would he wait half a decade to come after them?

Unless their plan had actually worked—for a time, anyway. They'd hoped that inhabiting humans would be like donning camouflage. That it would make them invisible to other supernatural entities who might wish to do to them what their captor had. But maybe he had crossed with them, after all. Perhaps it had simply taken him this long to figure out what they'd done and where they were hiding.

If he had followed them, and if their captor did find them, then Sia had way more to worry about than a communication barrier.

"What are you doing?" a smooth, deep voice asked from behind her.

Sia spun around, fear and guilt seizing her lungs, though she couldn't fathom what she had to feel guilty about. She clutched her phone to her chest, her gaze darting about. Because that surely was a great look on her. "Nothing," she said after a moment. "What are you doing?"

Donovan's dark lashes lowered over irises shimmering softly in the streetlamp's light as he studied her. He tilted his head to one side, causing a lock of dark hair to fall over his brow. "Is everything okay, Doc?"

Forcing a smile at that point in her life was like peeling taffy that had melted and then cooled again off her car dashboard, but she finally managed to do it. "Of course. Why wouldn't it be?" She tried to cross her arms over her chest and lean against a stack of crates. She failed and almost landed face-first on the pavement.

He rushed forward, but she caught herself and smoothed a hand over her hair. "How's Elwyn?" she asked, deflecting. Her cheeks burned, and she thanked the powers for low light. Blushing was another human trait she despised.

After a long moment, Donovan lifted a shoulder. "You'd know better than me, you being her medic and all."

Medic. Wasn't that a military term? Had he served? Donovan had been the first member of the group she'd met when she walked up to the main house of the Loehr's compound, the one constructed to keep Charley's daughter safe. Knowing that Charley wasn't around to contest her proclamation, Sia had pretended to be a friend of Charley's from school. She'd told them that Charley had asked her to keep an eye on Elwyn and offered her services. A man named Garrett Swopes, another of Elwyn's guardians, had hired her on the spot as Donovan watched their interaction.

Coincidentally, Donovan was also the first of the ragtag team she'd treated when he laid down his bike to avoid getting beheaded by a truck that had pulled out in front of him. And yet, even after all these years, she still knew so little about him.

Her phone pinged, and she read the text from Benji. *Run, Sia. And believe nothing.*

She sucked in a sharp breath and whirled away from Donovan to tap on her phone screen. She tried calling Benji yet again, but it went straight to voicemail. Before she knew it, she was rushing around the building, stumbling through dark shadows and over uneven ground. She tripped twice but managed to catch herself both times.

Would Charley's barrier keep Kursch out? She just didn't know, and she couldn't risk him finding Elwyn. The daughter of two gods would be like heroin for a soul eater like Kursch. She would be a drug he would never be able to resist. And her energy was so powerfully bright, hot, and pure, he could live off Charley's daughter for eons.

"Doc?" Donovan called out, but she was running on fumes and blind panic. She didn't have time to explain. She needed to put as much distance between herself and Elwyn as she could. Her worst nightmare must've come true. And that thought squeezed her chest so tightly that the edges of her vision blurred.

She'd planned for this moment for a long time. They all had. Determining what they would do if Kursch somehow managed to find them. They all had contingency plans but thought there would be some kind of warning. A sign or advance notice. How had Kursch stopped them from communicating? Prohibited them from alerting each other?

Not that it mattered now. Charley and her husband had created a barrier over Santa Fe and the surrounding area to keep nefarious entities from entering. They'd done it to keep their daughter safe. But again, would it work on Kursch? Would the barrier keep him out?

She could only hope it would because surely Kursch would be able to sense an entity as powerful as Elwyn Loehr.

Sia scrambled into her crossover and started it just as Donovan appeared from around the building. He stepped into the low light, his broad shoulders tense and looking like they carried the weight of the world. He scraped a hand through thick, black hair in desperate need of a trim as she peeled out of the parking lot. She watched him in the rearview, worried it would be for the last time. Then, realizing it very well could be, she slammed on the brakes, threw the car into park, and jumped out of the vehicle.

His gaze followed her as she ran up to him, and though he had his brows drawn tightly in concern, he stood his ground, waiting to see what she planned. When she stopped short, he only studied her, waiting patiently for her next move. Then he did the hair thing again, his shirtsleeve stretched tight around his thick biceps. And that was her undoing.

She stepped even closer, and he dropped his hand. "In case I never see you again."

"Why wouldn't you—?"

Before he could finish his sentence, she threw her arms around his neck and planted her mouth on his.

It was her first kiss—and most likely her last. But, still, it was her first. And it was wonderful. A spark of electricity arced through her at the contact, and she suddenly understood the popularity.

Donovan didn't hesitate. He pulled her closer, his large hands sliding around to her back and molding her body to his. And for the first time since becoming human, Sia was grateful for the curves she'd inherited. They fit nicely against him as he angled his head to deepen the kiss, his tongue urging her lips apart.

She parted her lips with a soft moan and pressed into him even more. He tasted sweet and smooth, his mouth opening wider as he demanded more of her, and she realized that he was enjoying their interaction as much as she was.

Her phone pinged again, and it was like someone had poured ice water down the back of her blouse. She gasped and pushed away from him, covering her mouth with one hand in horror. "I am so sorry. I didn't mean... I have to go."

But he didn't seem angry. And he looked more intrigued than disappointed. "Where are you going in such a hurry?" Had his voice gotten deeper? Huskier? Sexier?

She felt warmth spread through her nether regions as her phone pinged once more. "I'm sorry," she said again, sobering. She turned and ran for the red crossover idling half in and half out of the parking lot. Then she looked back over her shoulder and lied. "I'll explain later!"

She had no idea if there would be a later. Or if she would ever see him again. But at least now she could die happy.

Chapter Three

It got awkward, and then
I made it worse somehow.
—An autobiography

Donovan watched the doctor move through her house from the cover of his Ford Raptor. After decades of *all Harleys, all the time*, having an actual interior for these types of situations helped to keep his spirits up.

He left the bar in the capable hands of his best friends and a sassy imp named Charley. Then he offered up a quick prayer that it would still be standing when he got back. Trouble tended to follow Charley Davidson around like a bad habit—probably why he liked her so much.

Unfortunately, he liked the doc's kiss more. She'd surprised him. They'd been at that stage of a relationship that hovered somewhere between professional acquaintances and almost-friends for five years, but she'd never seemed particularly interested in him. Thus, he'd kept his distance. And then the kiss. One that'd shaken him more than he wanted to admit.

He rubbed his mouth unconsciously as he thought about it. It was like she'd never kissed a man before in her life. First, she hadn't closed her eyes. At least, not right away. She'd kept her hazel irises trained on him as though to gauge his reaction. As if worried that he wouldn't welcome the attention she was lavishing on him. She needn't have been concerned. To say that his interest bordered on *thundering* would be an understatement.

Second, she hadn't opened her mouth. Not until he'd coaxed her to do so. She'd literally just put her lips on his and waited. Yet she'd seemed to enjoy even that much. She sank against him, her curves molding to his body so thoroughly that it'd stolen his breath.

He'd kept his gaze locked with hers until her lids finally fluttered shut, and her lips parted. No matter how hard he'd tried not to be moved, his efforts had proven fruitless. Her scent had him reeling. He'd always been fascinated by it. A combination of sweet and sensual, tropics and spice, the unusual fragrance saturated his clothes every time she came within five feet of him. And she had been much closer than that for the kiss.

His pants tightened around his hips at the thought. But when he'd wrapped her in his arms, he'd instantly regretted the response his body always had when she was near. Apparently, his mind had yet to crawl out of the gutter it'd come from. She'd trembled, and he'd felt the rapid pounding of her heart as it tried to fight its way out of her chest. Something terrible had happened, and yet there he'd stood, groping her like a sixth-grader who'd just entered puberty. Classy.

The doc was part of the family now. She'd seen things that no one else on Earth had but never questioned any of it. He supposed it was because she had gone to school with Charley. She must've known about Charley's abilities, at least a little, because nothing seemed to faze the doc—even when Elwyn went missing at five years old and came back three days later as a teenager. The doc had taken it all in stride. Perhaps a little too much in stride.

Donovan watched as she knelt in her dining room and pried up some wooden slats from the floor, her movements rushed with panic. Thankfully, she'd left the blinds open in her front window, giving Donovan an unobstructed view of her erratic behavior.

He thought about texting Teacup to see if she had any insight into the doc's dilemma, but it was late, and even gods who subsisted on coffee and sarcasm—truly her mother's daughter—needed their beauty sleep.

The doc finally pulled up enough boards to drag out a satchel. She took it to her dining room table and opened it. Though Donovan couldn't see inside, people only hid three things in their floors: money, damning evidence, or an emergency bug-out bag. Since he didn't take the doc for a serial killer, and she probably had access to plenty of money with her being a doctor and all, bug-out bag it was. It could contain any number of items, most notably emergency cash, fake IDs, a burner phone, and possibly even a weapon.

She'd showered and changed into jeans and a white button-down when she got home. Her damp hair fell softly around her shoulders as she worked. She closed the satchel and then glanced around her house as though performing a final check. Seeming satisfied, she pulled on a black hoodie and grabbed her coffee, a small suitcase with rollers, and the satchel before heading to her car.

When she tripped in her driveway and landed hard on her knees and palms, his hand shot to his door handle, but he stopped himself. His gut clenched as he watched her struggle to her feet, but he needed to know what was going on. Where she was headed. Donovan figured he was probably the last person she would trust with her problems. They hardly knew each other. So, he decided to follow her and assess the situation while keeping his distance. Unless she needed him, of course.

She recovered and drove to a gas station. He followed and looked on as she fought the card reader for what seemed like five minutes. She finally got it to work, and he took out his phone as she filled up.

What did he really know about the doc? She'd shown up on the Loehrs' doorstep five years ago, very soon after Charley and her husband *ascended*, as they called it. They'd focused all their energy on creating a haven for their daughter while the rest of the Earth-bound got the compound ready. Elwyn Loehr was surrounded by people who loved her enough to risk their lives for her—and her cause, of course. Being the subject of prophecies claiming that she would defeat Satan and save humankind could not be an easy burden to bear, but the kid handled it with the grace and smart mouth of a true professional. Donovan knew that Charley was insanely proud of her daughter. Hell, *he* was insanely proud of her daughter. But the doc had shown up barely a month after a group of body-snatching demons almost caused a global apocalypse.

She was a real doctor. There was no doubt about that. And she'd said that she'd gone to school with Charley. That she knew about the peculiar events that followed Charley everywhere she went. But had anyone actually checked? Surely, Swopes, one of Charley's best friends and the man she'd left in charge of her daughter's care, had run a background check.

Donovan did a quick search of the doc's name: Lucia Mirabal. The usual stuff came up—her credentials, her volunteer work, the hospital where she'd worked until she accepted the job with the Loehrs—the couple currently raising Elwyn, and Farrow's human parents.

He took note of the date she'd left the hospital. It had been right around the time the demon horde was trying to make Earth its bitch. They were like leeches, and the hospitals had been overrun. Maybe, after everything that had happened, the doc decided to take a break from the medical facility and seek out other opportunities. Seeing all those people come down with a mysterious illness that no one—not even to this day—could explain had probably shaken her. A strange near-apocalypse tended to change people.

But another article caught his eye. He scrolled to a news post. The headline read: *Local Doctor Attacked in Alley.* The doc's professional headshot, a picture he'd loved since first seeing it, topped the article. He paused a moment to admire the doc's red hair and ethereal—a word he'd never used before meeting her—features before continuing to the article. After reading it, he sat, stewing in his shock, so deep in thought that he almost missed the doc pulling onto St. Francis.

He hurried after her while trying to read the article at the same time, swerving twice to avoid oncoming traffic. No one had ever accused him of having an overabundance of common sense.

According to the reporter, the attack happened close to the hospital where the doc had been employed. She'd been to dinner with friends but had parted ways with them outside the restaurant. A witness told police that she went into the alley alone. No one had dragged her. Had she heard something? Had someone called out to her?

Whatever the case, at the time of print, they'd yet to identify her attacker. All Donovan knew was that they had taken her to Presbyterian, which was a hotspot for the demonic activities of the time. He thanked the powers that be that she'd made it out of that hospital alive.

Had one of the demons attacked her? They'd certainly left enough carnage in their wake to warrant suspicion. Even the most peace-loving humans the demons inhabited became violent. No, not just violent. Enraged. The whole situation was straight out of Hollywood.

And the timing fit. Her attack had occurred right smack-dab in the middle of those screwed-up days. If Charley hadn't come back from whatever hell dimension she'd been sent to, there was no telling what the world would look like today. If that'd happened, though, whatever or whoever she was running from was not her attacker. As far as he knew, no more of those demons were left on the plane. Maybe she wasn't running *from* so much as running *to*. She'd gotten a call. Perhaps someone needed her help. But why would she have said what she did: *in case I never see you again?*

He simply had no way of knowing what was going on until they reached her destination, and his head hurt just thinking about it.

He followed the doc south out of Santa Fe, and for the first couple of hours, he tried to read and drive at the same time, searching for clues on what'd become of her attacker. Sadly, there was nothing. He found no evidence of an arrest or conviction. Was the assailant never caught?

Two and a half hours into their trip, he began to worry that she would realize he was following her, but he tried to stay back far enough to compensate for that. He plugged the charger into his quickly dying phone and then went into his contacts. He found the name he was searching for and pressed call.

Garrett Swopes, Elwyn's primary guardian, picked up after only two rings. Donovan was almost impressed.

"This'd better be good," Swopes said, his voice groggy. Donovan looked at the time. Twelve after midnight.

"Am I disturbing your beauty sleep?" he asked the man.

"Something like that."

"My bad," he offered by way of an apology, not in the least bit concerned. "What do you know about the doc?"

He heard Swopes stir as though sitting up in bed. "What do you mean?"

"She was attacked before she came to work for us. Do you know what happened?"

In the background, Donovan heard a feminine voice, thick with sleep. "Did something happen? Is Elwyn okay?"

"Sorry to cause alarm," Donovan said, finally feeling a tug of guilt for, well... causing alarm.

"Everything is fine," Swopes said. "Come here."

"I can't," Donovan said. "I'm in pursuit." He heard a soft sigh as, presumably, Marika settled next to Swopes.

"What is this about, St. James?" Swopes only sounded annoyed for his fiancée's benefit. Donovan could hear the piqued interest in his voice.

"Your charge has me watching the doc. She's worried about her. Said she's been distraught, and I have to concur. Something is definitely up. Do you know what might have the doc so riled? Or why Elwyn is so concerned?"

"That little shit didn't tell me anything."

"You can't call her that," Marika said, her tone admonishing, and Donovan couldn't help but grin. Swopes had met his match. Served him right.

"Sorry," Swopes said sheepishly. "I don't know a thing. You're following the doc now?"

"I am. It looks like we're headed for Ruidoso. Maybe farther. Do you know if she has family in that area?"

"Not that I know of. She only has her mother, and she's in a nursing home in Albuquerque. But what's this about an attack?"

"Who was attacked?" Marika asked in a rush.

"The doc."

"Oh, my God!"

"No, don't get up." Swopes tried to calm his soon-to-be. "Here, I'll put this on speaker."

"Okay."

Donovan waited for her to get settled again before explaining. "I saw an article. The doc was attacked in an alley around the time the leeches tried to take over the world."

"You mean the shade demons?" Swopes asked.

"Seriously? I have to be PC when it comes to the blood-sucking monsters that killed Charley's sister?"

"Not at all. I just wanted to clarify. Now that I know what we're talking about, I can answer your question. No, I had no idea the doc had been attacked before we met her. Are you sure it was one of the possessed?"

"No. And that's the problem. I can't find anything about an arrest. There was so much going on at that time. Maybe the cops chalked it up to a psycho and called it a day."

"Maybe."

"Is that what has the doc riled?" Marika asked.

"I don't know, but she grabbed a bug-out bag and ran."

"No shit?" she asked, astonished.

Donovan almost laughed. He'd never heard Marika swear. Then again, he'd never heard her say much of anything. She and Swopes had a son together whom they shared custody of, but they'd only recently rekindled the spark in their relationship. Thus, Donovan rarely saw the woman, much less talked to her. "No shit," he answered. "I was just wondering how thorough of a background check your fiancé did on her."

"I thought *you* ran the background," Swopes said.

"Why would I? Isn't that *your* job?"

"I was a little busy getting the compound ready for the dark princess."

"You can't call her that either," Swopes' intended said.

Donovan liked Marika. "So, we really don't know if the doc went to school with Charley or if Charley asked her to keep an eye on Elwyn?"

"I guess not."

"Come to think of it, we don't really know anything about her."

"We know one thing," Swopes said. "We know she's a damned good doctor, and we know she doesn't ask questions about our... extracurricular activities."

"That's two things. And I agree. But something has her spooked. And if I didn't know better, I'd say we might be short a medic. I don't think she plans to come back."

Chapter Four

I may look fine, but deep down
I don't remember any of my passwords.
—Meme

Believe nothing. What did that even mean? What was Benji trying to tell her?

Sia had forgotten how long it took to get to Ruidoso from Santa Fe. She managed to shave half an hour off the trip by incorporating a loose interpretation of the posted speed limits, but she was still on the verge of a complete mental breakdown by the time she hit the Capitan Pass. Only a few more miles, and she'd be at Benji's house. Or his human parents' house, rather. But even being this close to him, she couldn't hear him. Not that proximity mattered. As with every plane they'd ever been on, they'd always been able to hear each other, no matter the distance. But it seemed even quieter now. Darker. Colder.

The Capitan Pass was full of sharp curves and steep drop-offs. She had no choice but to slow down. She checked her rearview for the ten-thousandth time and caught a glimpse of headlights. That wasn't abnormal. Not in the least. It was the fact that a similar set had appeared and disappeared throughout her entire trip. Almost as though the person behind her was purposely slowing down and then speeding back up to check on her whereabouts.

But why would they? She rolled her eyes and gripped the steering wheel tighter, growing more paranoid by the second. No one was following her. If Kursch had found his way onto this plane and had somehow located the others, he would not be driving a vehicle and following her at a safe distance. No. If Kursch had found them, they would all be dead. Or worse, taken back to the void.

Her stomach clenched hard at the thought. She'd prefer death. For all she knew, her friends actually *had* been taken back. Her stomach hurt just thinking about it. It was a very unwelcome side effect of—for all intents and purposes—being human. Even with the vast knowledge of the woman she'd inhabited, it had taken Sia a long time to adjust to life within a framework of flesh and bone. And physical pain from an emotional event took longer to acclimate to than she'd hoped. She'd always thought the visceral reaction odd, even with the medical knowledge she'd gained.

The headlights disappeared from her rearview as she flew around curves and up the steep grades of the mountain. She came to a series of tight turns and slowed, veering left, right, then left again.

Concentrating on the road helped her anxiety. She'd tried to get ahold of Benji at least fifty times, to no avail. The mindless monotony of driving was oddly comforting. At least until the headlights reappeared a moment later, only much closer this time. The brightness in her mirror blinded her for a split second. Just long enough for her to misjudge the degree of curvature required for her next turn.

She'd done the math. She was very good at it. But the lights had thrown her, and a heartbeat before she realized what was happening, she found her right tires hovering off the side of the mountain. She screamed and jerked the wheel, overcorrecting and almost pitching her Toyota over the side. Instead, she ended up veering into the opposite lane. Thankfully, it was the middle of the night with nary a car in sight—except for the one on her ass.

Whoever it was slowed down and gave her some breathing room once she recovered, but she kept her eye on them. The turnoff to Benji's house was up ahead, so she put on her blinker and glared into her rearview. "Don't you even think about following me."

She turned left, going higher on the mountain, but kept a vigilant watch on the lights behind her. The car stayed its course, speeding past her once she'd cleared the intersection. The tension that had been coiled between her shoulder blades, cinching them tighter, eased a bit.

She drew in a deep breath and searched through the darkness for the next turn. "You're losing it, Sia. Just stay focused."

The near-accident was her fault. She'd been so lost in thought that she hadn't slowed down enough. And her paranoia had convinced her that someone was following her. She had to remember who she was dealing with. Kursch would cut her throat and wait for her to exit the human body so he could kill her with a grin on his face. Well, if he *had* a face.

A mutilated white mailbox came into view with the name *Henderson* stenciled on the side. It was more faded than she remembered, and she'd just visited Benji a few months ago. She took a right and eased up the narrow, tree-lined drive.

The Hendersons had a tiny cabin with very few amenities, but it was Mr. Henderson's pride and joy. *"Completely self-sufficient,"* the rascally man would say with a laugh. Benji had found such an amazing family. A mom, dad, and two little sisters who thought their big brother had hung the moon. Sia envied Benji that—the closeness he shared with his family. The dynamics. He truly embodied the role of the human he inhabited. Having all of the kid's memories, Benji was the only one out of the lot of them—seven to be exact—who really embraced human life and welcomed it with open arms. He fought with his sisters yet protected them with every ounce of strength he had. He disobeyed his parents, then apologized and doubled down on his chores to make up for it. He enjoyed being human so much, Sia was surprised that he hadn't severed contact with the rest of them years ago. In some ways, they were merely a reminder of the horrible past they shared.

She stopped short and turned off her headlights, not wanting to wake anyone. What if all of this was a mistake? What if Benji was fine? Maybe someone had stolen his phone and was punking her. Wasn't that what they called it?

After a quick glance at the satchel, she decided against bringing it along. It was one thing to sneak up to a dark house in the middle of the night. It was another thing altogether to sneak up to a dark house in the middle of the night carrying a wicked-looking iron dagger. They didn't even know for certain if iron would work on Kursch, but it was the only weapon they had.

Praying she was overreacting, she killed the engine, grabbed her phone—mainly for the flashlight feature—and stepped out of the car. The familiar scent of pine washed over her, and she took comfort in it. But before she took two steps, a twig snapped nearby. She froze and slowly raised her phone, but her flashlight was hardly a match for the blackness of a forest at night. It barely penetrated five feet into the shadowy thickness.

She waited with bated breath, listening with her whole body for another sound. When none came, she ventured forth. She only stumbled once, and that was due to a pothole the size of Texas in the drive. That thing would've bottomed out her poor Toyota, and it had been through enough for one night.

The cabin seemed way more ominous at night. It sat in complete darkness, shadows on top of shadows, which Sia found odd. Mr. Henderson had always kept a porch light on, as well as a floodlight with a motion sensor. Sia's approach should have triggered it.

Growing warier by the second, she ignored the fact that the hand holding her phone suddenly shook uncontrollably and crept to the side of the cabin where Benji's room was located. She stole up to the window and shined her light inside. What she saw paralyzed her lungs and sent chills racing up her spine. Not because Benji was inside. And not because he wasn't. But because there was *nothing* inside.

Trash and old clothes littered the floor, along with a broken chair and a dirty mattress that looked like it had served time in a drug den. Graffiti covered the walls, and the curtains that Benji's mom had made the last time Sia visited hung like a tattered testament to the forgotten artifacts. The room looked like it hadn't been lived in for years, but she had just been here three months ago.

She reeled back and tried to take in the rest of the house. The trim Mr. Henderson had painted last summer had cracked, and large chunks had peeled off.

This couldn't be. She had *just* been here for Benji's parents' anniversary party.

The ground suddenly became her enemy as she tried to traverse it without tripping. She stumbled up the steps to the front door. It sat open, dirt and leaves creating a path to the inside. Mrs. Henderson worked tirelessly to keep her tiny house clean, and the front porch was her sanctuary. She had a small area where she sat while drinking tea and watching the birds. And then there was the porch swing Mr. Henderson had built for her. It now hung lopsidedly on its chains, one side broken and the other barely hanging on for dear life. The bench looked centuries old, and several slats had been damaged, the wood splintered and scraggly. Sia had never been more confused in her entire life.

She followed the debris inside and saw more of the same, along with a couple of raccoons and the blur of a mouse scampering across the cluttered floor. Utterly bewildered, Sia stared for a solid ten minutes, a thousand scenarios rushing through her mind. Not a single one made sense. After what seemed like a week, she turned to go back to her car. The chill of the night air was getting to her, though it was probably the only thing keeping her from losing consciousness. When she turned, she found herself staring down the double barrels of a shotgun.

She dropped her phone and stumbled back, unable to look past the two circles pointed straight at her face.

"And just what do you think you're doing there, missy?" It was the voice of an older woman, hoarse and scratchy as though she'd smoked unfiltered for her whole life.

"I was looking for the Hendersons," Sia said, keeping her palms held high. She retreated another step, but the doorframe stopped her from going far.

"I've been keeping an eye on this place since the locals decided it was party central."

"I'm not a local. I'm just a friend of the Hendersons."

"Got that name off the mailbox, did ya?"

"No," Sia said. "I come here all the time."

The woman snorted. "Well, you're either a very bad liar, or you got the wrong house. Ain't sure which, considering you don't look like a druggie."

"I'm not, I assure you. I'm a doctor." Not that she had any way to prove that while standing on the porch.

"No shit?"

"Can I get my phone?"

The silhouette nodded, so Sia sank down and grabbed her cell before rising again, hands held up for good measure. "I can show you my CV. And I have a card in my bag." She pointed one finger from around the phone toward her car. "Can we, perhaps, rethink the shotgun thing?"

"Can we, perhaps, rethink the flashlight?" the woman said, squinting at Sia.

Sia finally got a look at the woman. Gray hair pulled back into a wiry bun, a ruddy complexion on a round face, and overalls with a plaid shirt underneath.

"Oh, of course." Sia swiped her phone and turned off the flashlight before raising her hands again. Unfortunately, the woman didn't hold up her end of the bargain, keeping the shotgun trained in the direction of her face. Sia decided not to press the issue. "Do you know where the Hendersons went? Their house looks abandoned."

"Sharp as a tack, you are. Like I said, you're going to have to come up with something better than that."

Sia shook her head. "I don't understand what you mean."

"Look, princess, the Hendersons ain't lived here going on five years."

"That—that's not possible," Sia said, fighting the urge to hyperventilate.

"Come to think of it," the woman continued, "no one's lived here for five years. This cabin was tied up in all kinds of legal hullabaloo. No idea what ever came of that, but it's been abandoned since their son died."

Sia felt the bones in her legs dissolve. "Benji? But he didn't die. He was rescued and resuscitated."

"Only in the Hendersons' dreams. He died five years ago almost to the day."

The world tilted under Sia's feet, and the woman reaffirmed her willingness to shoot her where she stood by repositioning the shotgun on her shoulder and lowering her head as though looking at Sia through a scope—not that she would need anything of the sort at this distance.

A male voice came to them from the trees. "There you are."

The woman swung the shotgun toward the voice as a man walked out of the forest. "Sorry, I got turned around," he said, and Sia immediately recognized the voice. Donovan St. James. But how? "Whoa," he said, spotting the shotgun. He showed his palms and stopped immediately. "No need for that. We come in peace."

"Like I haven't heard that before."

"We were just looking for the Hendersons."

The woman seemed to bristle and maybe even grow a little nervous. She shifted her weight but never took her eyes off Donovan.

"What are you doing here?" Sia asked, panic flooding her chest and making it difficult to breathe.

"I said I'd meet you. I know I'm late, but damn." He looked at the woman and shook his head. "That's always been my problem with women. I'm very forgettable."

Holy cow, did he ever have that wrong. "Donovan, you need to leave."

"What?" he said, disappointment evident on his face. She didn't miss the fact that he was slowly making his way closer to them. "You told me I could finally meet the Hendersons."

"And I told her," the woman said, "the Hendersons ain't lived here in five years."

He nodded and looked around the cabin, stepping onto the first stair. "Welp, I'd say that makes you a liar, then."

Sia sucked in a soft breath. Did he know something she didn't?

The woman tsked and lowered the gun a couple of centimeters as he took yet another stair, inching closer to them. She grinned at him and, right before pulling the trigger, said, "I suppose it does."

Chapter Five

English is a great language.
For example, "take out" can mean food, dating, or murder.
—True fact

Donovan thought about Sia as he walked. The doc lacked basic social skills as if she didn't know how to behave in certain situations. Not that there was anything wrong with that, but it could explain why she refrained from speaking when they were all together. Seriously, though, a woman with her looks? How could she not be a social butterfly?

Donovan knew, of course, that looks didn't automatically create a stunning social intellect, but the two often went hand-in-hand. Sia seemed to suffer from crippling shyness, and it only endeared him to her more.

Those were the shiny gems he thought about as he trekked through the forest closer to where he'd seen the doc park her car. Marika had offered to call Sia to maybe figure out what was going on, but he'd asked her to hold that thought. He wanted to see where this particular rabbit hole led, so he requested that Marika give him a day. Now maybe he would get some answers.

He'd pulled off the road about half a mile back and jogged until he spotted her crossover halfway up a drive. Then he used the vehicle as cover, darting into the forest once he reached it to flank her for a better view. And there she was, even her silhouette alluring. She'd certainly been blessed with impressive curvatures, but really. That kiss. He couldn't stop thinking about it and how inexperienced the doc had seemed.

"That—that's not possible."

He heard the astonishment in Sia's voice and crept closer, making sure the trees offered him enough cover to approach unseen. He listened as a woman spoke about the cabin's previous occupants. Though he couldn't hear every word, he caught enough to know that what the woman said stressed the doc out.

Sia picked up her phone, and Donovan finally realized why she had been standing with her hands in the air—the woman held a shotgun on her. A blind rage consumed him instantly. Naturally, he'd left his pistol in the truck, but he didn't waste a moment. He stepped out of the cover of the trees and said as casually as he could, "There you are."

The woman swung the shotgun toward him, as expected.

"Sorry, I got turned around," he said, taking in as much of the doc's demeanor as he could. She was not having a good day. Her chest rose and fell in short bursts, but he couldn't worry about that right now. He pretended that he'd just seen the shotgun and raised his hands. "Whoa. No need for that. We come in peace."

"Like I haven't heard that before."

So, either the woman was an alien enthusiast or on just enough medication to make her paranoid. "We were just looking for the Hendersons."

The woman shifted to get a better view of him.

That's right. Keep your attention right here. He took another step closer.

"What are you doing here?" Sia asked him, and the panic in her voice caused an odd reaction in him. Was she worried about him?

"I said I'd meet you. I know I'm late, but damn." He looked at the woman and shook his head. "That's always been my problem with women. I'm very forgettable."

"Donovan, you need to leave," the doc said, and he wanted to smile. She was actually worried about him. This might just be the best day of his life. At least, thus far.

"What?" he said, feigning disappointment as he took another step. "You told me I could finally meet the Hendersons."

"And I told her," the woman said, "the Hendersons ain't lived here in five years."

He nodded and studied the cabin, stepping onto the first stair, a few inches closer to Farmer Jane. The thing was, he'd looked up the area before traversing into the unknown. Once he saw the name on the broken mailbox, a quick Google search gave him what he needed.

According to the city registrar and an article Donovan had found about the most recent Aspen Festival—where Mr. Henderson had sold carvings at a booth just a month prior—the Hendersons were not only still in the area, they also still lived at that cabin. And their son, Benji, was still very much alive. At least as of a few weeks ago. So, how did the cabin look utterly abandoned? And what had Farmer Jane done with the doc's friends?

"Welp," he said, figuring it was time to call her out, "I'd say that makes you a liar, then."

The doc gasped softly at his words, hope evident on her shadowy features.

The woman tsked and dropped the barrel until it was pointed squarely at his chest. He took another stair with every intention of tackling her to the ground when she grinned at him.

It was at that moment that he knew he was fucked.

"I suppose it does," she said, right before pulling the trigger.

Luckily, he saw it coming. Unluckily, he was not Charley Davidson. He could not slow time to get out of the way of a speeding bullet. And he damned sure wasn't faster than a shotgun blast. She must've lowered the barrel even more right before pulling because the pellets hit his left arm and the side of his midsection so hard that it dropped him to his knees. But not for long. In the time it took her to pull the trigger a second time, he was on her.

The doc fell back as he tackled the woman to the ground and put her in a headlock from behind, wrapping his legs around her waist. They struggled for a few seconds, the pain almost making him black out, but when she raised the shotgun and pointed it at Sia, he had no choice. He put all his strength behind his hold and snapped the woman's neck.

The problem was, he didn't know if that would stop her. Clearly, something about her was supernatural. The woman he held against him was as cold as ice and smelled like embalming fluid. Zombies were above his paygrade. And fuck zombies. That was where he drew the line. What the hell had the doc gotten herself into?

He waited as the woman sank against him, and then he waited some more. After a long moment, he glanced at the doc. She sat huddled against the cabin, watching wide-eyed, her terrified gaze seeming to follow something he couldn't see. She scrambled back and guarded her face with an arm as though readying for an attack.

"Doc?" he said, barely able to breathe. He rolled the woman off him and slid to Sia's side, but her gaze shot to the left as though watching something leave in a hurry. After that, she relaxed. A little. "Doc, what the actual fuck?" he ground out from between gritted teeth.

She gaped and him then stood so she could tower over him. "What are you doing here? Why would you be here? Did you follow me? Was that you?" She didn't wait for an answer. She whirled around and held up her phone, clearly hoping for a bar to appear. "I knew it. I knew someone was following me, but did I listen to my gut? Of course not."

He'd tried to get service while traipsing through the forest. He'd had it on the road and at the end of the driveway, but once he got closer to the Hendersons' cabin, there was nothing.

"Why would I do something as inane as listen to my gut?"

"The princess of the underworld sent me," he said, referring back to an earlier inquiry. In his defense, he didn't figure he could answer many of them. The doc seemed to be having a moment. When she whirled back around to question him with what he assumed was a glare—it was too dark to know for certain—he elaborated. "Little miss Loehr."

"Beep? I mean, Elwyn?" she corrected.

Admittedly, most of the people at the compound still called the kid Beep. He found it adorable, which was probably why he never called her that. He didn't do adorable. He did cool. Rugged. Manly. Not at that exact moment, but under normal circumstances, he was like Marlon Brando and Sam Elliot's love child. At least, he liked to think so. But it was hard to be cool when catching your breath felt like swallowing razorblades.

"Elwyn asked you to follow me?"

"She asked me to keep an eye on you. Said you've seemed distraught. And I'd like to second that."

"I bet you would." She held up her phone again, and he felt they had more pressing matters than checking messages.

"What are you doing?" he asked since she had yet to help him up.

"We need an ambulance."

"Isn't that what you're for?"

She dropped her arm and did the gaping thing again. "You've been shot."

"Yes, but it was only rock salt."

She knelt beside him and shined the light on his wound. "So, it's not bad?"

"Oh, hell no. It's still bad. It's really bad. It's just not quite *as* bad as it could've been. Also, my jacket helped."

"Is it bulletproof?"

"Almost. It's leather. Can you help me up?"

"Wait, we need to stop the bleeding."

"We need to get to my truck."

"Why?"

"I have a gun there. Will that thing inside her come back?"

"I don't know. Either way, a gun won't help."

He'd figured as much. Because that would be too easy. "Fucking leeches."

"Leeches?" she asked.

"Those demon fucks who take over humans' bodies. There's nothing worse."

"Oh."

Even in his state of agonizing pain, he didn't miss the fact that she'd dropped her gaze as though suddenly self-conscious. Yet another puzzle to solve. But for now, they needed to get to a motel. Not a hotel, but a motor inn where they could park right at their door. He didn't want to explain a suspicious trail of blood to a night clerk eking out a living at the DoubleTree.

"Right," she said. "Leeches. Those are the worst."

"So, maybe a little help?"

She snapped back to him. "Wait, what about that woman? We... we killed her."

"Nah. I'm pretty sure she's been dead for a while now."

"How do you know?"

"Because I now have to wash the alluring scent of embalming fluid out of my hair. That's how."

The doc crinkled her nose, and it was too adorable—or it would have been if he did adorable.

An hour later, Donovan could hardly see clearly, much less walk straight. The pain that ripped through his midsection like red-hot pokers repeatedly doubled him over as he stumbled to the door of the motel room the doc had rented. He had to stop and wonder if the shotgun shells had been filled with some kind of magic fairy dust that caused extra agony to the receiver. Did the supernatural realm have such things?

Donovan did know one thing for certain, though. The doc had a lot of explaining to do.

"Seriously?" he said, ignoring the whine in his voice. "You couldn't get a room on the first floor?"

"Serves you right." Her voice was strained as she did her best to heft him up the concrete steps. "You shouldn't have followed me."

They'd had to leave his truck by the cabin and come into Ruidoso for a motel room. It was a sore spot. Another one. He loved his truck. Not as much as his Harley, but still. His other sore spot—or series of them—throbbed with a pain he never knew existed. But he had a short attention span. He could've forgotten.

The salve to the agony pulsing through his body was the doc. She felt amazing. Soft curves and that silken red hair he would kill to touch. Not to mention the fact that she smelled incredible.

Five minutes and several near-catastrophes later, he lay on a mattress harder than Teacup's glare and decided to ask the doc to perform last rights.

She said no.

"Please."

"I'm not a priest."

"I'm not a Catholic."

"Your jacket is incredible. It stopped almost all of the rock salt."

"Still burns like a Charley Davidson comeback."

The doc didn't crack even the slightest hint of a smile. They'd stopped for supplies along the way, and she was all business. Like she had been the day he'd laid down his bike to avoid being decapitated—he just didn't think it would be a good look for him.

Her elegant brows crinkled as she poked and prodded. And her scent—that damned alluring fragrance that wafted around him like heroin—made him lightheaded. "You probably have a broken rib or two."

"They don't feel broken. They just feel cracked."

"Someday, you can explain the difference in how either of those feels to me."

"Will do," he said, his voice strained as she tried to coax a burning piece of rock salt out of his side. "Aren't those eyebrow tweezers?"

"You refused to go to the hospital. You get eyebrow tweezers."

"As long as you sterilized them."

"Oh, crap." She stopped and studied the small instrument. "I knew I forgot to do something."

"You're funny."

"And you're a jerk. I can't believe you did that."

"What?" he asked, completely offended. "Saved your ass?"

"I was doing fine."

He snorted and then winced as she went in again. "This is going to max out my sodium intake for the entire week."

A smile, at last. Not that he could see her full lips from behind her mask, but her eyes crinkled at the corners, and an emotion he hadn't felt in a long time swelled inside his chest. Pride, perhaps? Adoration? The desire to spike a football and do a victory dance?

"Care to tell me what happened back there?"

She paused in her ministrations but didn't look at him.

"I promise I can take it. Clearly, you have some kind of supernatural ability. You saw the leech, or whatever it was, leave that woman's body. Is that it? Are you psychic or something? Is that why you've never questioned what happens at the compound?"

She went back to work without answering.

"You know you can trust me, right? After all I've seen, nothing would surprise me."

She huffed out a soft laugh, causing the tweezers to slip.

He tensed as a spasm of pain shot through him.

Her gorgeous eyes rounded as she glanced up. "I'm sorry."

"Sorry enough to tell me what's going on?"

Her thick lashes fell over her irises again, and he felt the loss of that earthy, springtime gaze immediately.

"If I could, I would," she said softly, her words barely audible from behind the powder-blue mask.

He shifted, hunting for a better position. It didn't help. Nothing helped. He'd had cracked ribs before. They sucked and took weeks to heal. Which sucked even more. "After everything I've seen," he said, giving up his quest, "you think I can't handle it? Or do you just not trust me?"

She put the tweezers down with a sigh. "Maybe a little of both."

"Ah. So, getting shot for you didn't earn me any brownie points?"

After she studied him for a long moment, she said, "I think I got all the salt out, but a couple of those need stitches. Take a deep breath."

"Why?"

Before he knew what was going on, the doc poured a light brown solution over his wounds. It didn't burn as much as the salt had, but it was an odd combination of sting and ice. He almost shot up at the shock, but she put both hands on his shoulders and held him down.

When it continued burning, he tilted his head back and waited out the storm.

"Thank you," she said, so softly he almost didn't hear her over the blood thundering through his veins.

He filled his lungs, trying to slow his pulse, then opened his eyes. The doc was back at work, threading a surgical needle. "I know you didn't find that at the Chug-N-Jug."

"No. I always carry a medical kit."

"In case you have to randomly sew someone up on the street?"

She stopped and gave him her full attention. It was a powerful ploy to weaken him even further. It worked on a thousand levels. "Have you met your friends?" she asked, her tone implying that he would never be accepted into Mensa.

She had a good point.

"Drink."

She lifted a small plastic cup to his mouth, but he eyed it warily and asked, "Potassium cyanide?"

"Liquid Lortab."

"So close." He took the cup and drained the sweet liquid then eased back onto the pillow.

"Just a couple of stitches, then we'll be done."

He gave her a thumbs-up, amazed at how fast the painkiller was working.

She smoothed something warm over his ribs, and he hardly felt a thing. Except her hands. He hadn't forgotten those hands. Or what they stirred in him. She'd saved his life today. Due to his colorful past, he had serious concerns about going to a legit hospital, but she'd been there for him. It was no wonder she didn't trust him. He could hardly blame her. Still, he felt he deserved an explanation.

"I'm not going to lie," she said.

He grinned. "That'll be refreshing."

"You could have internal bleeding."

He lifted a shoulder, amazed that it didn't hurt. "Better than external. It's so hard to get blood out of clothes in this economy."

"I'll call for backup."

"You do that. This stuff is incredible, Doc. You should've given it to me an hour ago."

"Please tell Elwyn I'm sorry."

He tried to look at her, but his lids suddenly weighed more than his... Harley. "Sure thing," he said. Or tried to. He had no clue how coherent his words were as his tongue had taken a sick day.

"And I'm sorry for this, too."

He started to forgive her for whatever wrongdoing she'd imagined herself doing, but he felt her lips on his, cool and hot at the same time. Soft and firm. Sweet and bitter—or maybe that was the medicine. Either way, he tried to kiss back, but the warmth of oblivion lured him to the deep end of the universe, and he drowned in the scent of her there.

He wanted to tell her how he felt about her, but she leaned forward and whispered in his ear. "I wish I were your human."

Chapter Six

You are about to exceed the
limits of my medication.
—T-shirt

Donovan St. James. She'd never felt anything like him. He exuded a strange, animalistic kind of power. An allure she'd never seen in all the eons she'd existed in one form or another. In her defense, she'd been incorporeal during all but the last five years of those eons. But the man had a sultry prowess that had her yearning to be near him.

Damn her human body.

She had to find Benji. She needed to know if the being she'd thought of as a sibling was still alive. Maybe he was, and this was just another game.

Kursch's specialty was mental warfare. For his own pleasure, of course. He would reward them with gifts when he wanted to feed off their light, then he would take it all away and terrify them when he wanted to feed off the dark. But it was all mental. None of it had ever existed and it had taken them millennia to figure that out.

No, that wasn't true. They'd never figured it out. A god named Charley Davidson had. She'd opened their eyes to the fact that they were nothing but the soul eater's puppets. That he'd locked them in the void and had been living off their energy since damned near the beginning of time. And she'd taught them how to fight back.

They'd barely begun that fight when Charley was pulled out of the void. Those who could followed her before the portal closed. Sia had been one of the lucky ones, and she owed Charley everything—they all did. But now it looked like their awakening was all for nothing.

Had Kursch followed them, as well? Or had he simply found them on this plane when there were literally as many planes in existence as stars in the sky? If he had sought them out, it wasn't for the ka-zhouah. It wasn't for her or Benji or any of the others. They would be a mere side dish. Sia knew that. Kursch had gotten a taste of Charley when she was in the void and he wanted more.

Sia also knew that he would never let the god go again once he found her. If Charley were truly human now, she would be much safer. Sia hoped that much for her. Even so, there was Elwyn. She was just as powerful as her parents. Sia felt it every time she was near her. Raw, untamed energy churned like a nuclear power plant inside the girl. She was like a magnetar, this plane's most powerful type of star—a thousand times more powerful than Earth's sun.

Sia could not let the soul eater find her. The haven only worked when Elwyn was within it. She would have to leave its confines eventually, and if Kursch were anywhere on this plane, he would feel the girl immediately. He would destroy the world to get to her if that's what it took, just as he had with Sia and Benji's peaceful home world.

She took the highway, heading toward Roswell. From there, she would keep going until she hit I-40 East and eventually make her way to North Carolina. She had to physically check on the others, knowing this could all be a trap. With the soul eater's skill at warping reality, who knew if any of what she was seeing now was even real. She wouldn't put it past Kursch to dangle a delicacy like Donovan St. James in front of her. The feelings she had for the man bordered on sinful, and it was probably like nothing Kursch had ever tasted before. Therefore, putting as much distance as possible between her and Donovan was of the utmost importance, as well. He'd gotten lucky this time. He may not survive their next encounter with Kursch, and Sia would never forgive herself. If the iron dagger did not work on Kursch—and they had no idea if it would—she knew it would work on her. She would take her life before subjecting Donovan to the soul eater's whims.

She thought about trying to contact Benji again but realized that Kursch could be tracking them that way. Maybe that was why the others had gone dark. She wouldn't know for certain until she physically found them. If she did, they could come up with a plan together. There was a chance they could kill Kursch. It was an infinitesimal one, but it was better than none at all.

Once she was on the road, she called the one man she knew could prevent Donovan from trying to pursue her: Garrett Swopes. In some ways, he was Donovan's boss. At least when it came to Elwyn and her prophesied army. Donovan had to listen to him. She just prayed he would.

"This'd better be good," Garrett said when he picked up, his voice groggy with sleep.

"Donovan St. James is hurt."

"What?" Garrett asked, sounding fully awake now.

"He's in room 212 at the Motel 6 on Canyon Road in Ruidoso. I did what I could, but he needs X-rays."

"What happened?" he asked, his voice suddenly razor-sharp. She heard shuffling across the line, like he was already getting dressed.

A lump formed in her throat when she realized that she would never see these people again. They had become as much of a family to her as the ka-zhouah, and she would forever be grateful to Charley for that. "Please tell Elwyn it's been an honor knowing her."

"Doc?"

"I will love you all forever." She hung up before he could get any more information out of her. The less he knew, the better. Even if she wanted to, even if things were perfect in their world, she could never be with Donovan. He would see her as a parasite, a leech, having taken over a human body. It wouldn't matter that it was no longer being used or that she'd healed it instantly upon entering it. She couldn't bear to see any disgust directed toward her on his face. It would be her undoing.

Garrett called her back. She rejected the call and blocked his number just as she hit the main highway, leaving everything she loved behind.

* * * *

The pounding would not stop, no matter how much he begged. If he could figure out where it was coming from, he could kick the offender's ass—if he could find his way back to the world of the living, that was.

"I got it!" a female said from somewhere in the distance.

"How did you manage to get the room key?" A man. One with a very familiar voice.

"I told him my fiancé was in there with another woman, and I wanted to catch them red-handed."

"When the fuck did you and St. James get engaged?"

A giggle and then a clicking sound, followed by a light bright enough to illuminate a black hole. It hit Donovan square in the face, making him thankful that he wasn't a vampire.

"Yeah," the woman continued, "the cheating-fiancé trick doesn't work at the Marriott in Albuquerque, in case you were wondering."

"I'm not even going to ask how you know that."

"Probably for the best." A pair of warm hands stroked his face. "He's alive, at least."

"You had to caress his face to figure that out?"

"Apparently. We are engaged, after all. He's terribly handsome in that rugged, aging-biker kind of way."

Aging?

"I hadn't noticed," the man said. "There's more blood than I expected."

"It disturbs me that you expected blood at all."

"Yeah, well, comes with the job. St. James," the man said, much louder than Donovan felt was necessary. "Are you bleeding internally?"

Donovan tried to answer, but it came out as a croak, so he raised a middle finger instead.

"I think he's going to be fine," the woman said.

A phone rang, and the woman picked up as Donovan tried to pry his eyelids apart. What the actual fuck? Did the doc superglue them together? Speaking of the doc... "Where is she?" he managed to say.

Someone put a warm towel in the palm of his hand. "She took off, but not before she called us." Swopes. That made sense. The doc would know that Swopes could order him around. Donovan rarely listened, but he did like to order people around.

He pressed the towel to his face, then groaned and rubbed his eyes. "What happened?" he asked from behind the terrycloth.

The woman answered. Marika. "We were hoping you could tell us. Did you get shot?"

"I did. Rock salt. That shit hurts so much worse than you think it will."

"We picked up your truck on the way over," Swopes said with way more humor in his voice than Donovan felt was necessary.

"How did you manage to get into my truck?"

"Marika has a remarkable ability to convince people to do her bidding."

"It's a gift," she said.

Donovan laughed but instantly regretted it. He grabbed his ribs, realizing the doc had wrapped them as a wave of agony washed over him.

"Looks like she left you a party favor."

Donovan finally managed to pry open his lids, and Swopes pointed at a small plastic cup holding a clear liquid. It sat on the nightstand with a note that read: *Drink this*. "Fuck that," he said. "That stuff knocked me on my ass. She said it was liquid Lortab."

Swopes picked it up and sniffed. "I'm pretty sure she lied to you."

"She does that.

"Elwyn says hi," Marika said.

"I have a bone to pick with her."

"Oh, okay." She put her phone on speaker.

"Hey, Donovan," the precocious teen said as if she hadn't almost sent him to his death.

"What is she? And why me?" Oddly enough, he didn't have to explain. That told him he was on the right track, and Teacup knew more than she was letting on.

"I don't know what she is. Are you okay?"

"Don't change the subject."

She released a lengthy sigh that proved teens shared similar traits, no matter what plane they grew up on. "I *don't* know what she is, but I do know she's not... entirely human."

"What?" Swopes said, almost as shocked as Donovan. "What do you mean?"

"It's hard to explain."

"I've sensed it, too," Marika said.

"And you're just now telling me this?"

"It never came up before. She's definitely different, but I don't get demon vibes from her."

Elwyn agreed. "Me, neither. She's something else. Something... ethereal. Something beautiful."

Donovan couldn't agree more. "What's after her?"

"Something's after her?" Elwyn asked in alarm. "What kind of something?"

"I don't know, but it inhabited the body of a dead woman and tried to kill us with rock salt."

"That's a weird weapon of choice. So, not a demon, then. The rumors are true. They really do hate salt. I'm sorry, Donovan."

He instantly regretted the subtle sharpness of his tone. "Don't be. If you hadn't sent me to watch her, she could be dead right now."

"Do you know where she went?"

"No," he said, struggling to adjust the pillow at his back.

Marika reached over to help, but Swopes cut in and did it for her.

He fought a grin. "I know how to find her, though. First, I need one of you to do some digging for me."

"Oh! Me!" Elwyn said. "I can do it! Pick me!"

He pictured her waving an arm in the air as though trying to get her teacher's attention and laughed again. Oddly enough, it hurt just as bad as the first time.

"You have school," Swopes said. "And your grandmother is already mad at me for losing you for three days."

"She's not mad. She's just upset that she didn't get to see me grow up."

"I can't blame her." Swopes had been more disappointed in himself than anyone. Donovan had felt his remorse. But it wasn't like he could've done anything to prevent it. Elwyn had suddenly developed the nifty skill of jumping from plane to plane, using the souls of the departed as portals. Who knew a five-year-old would figure out how to do something so mindboggling?

"I can do research during study hour."

"Isn't study hour reserved for studying?" Swopes asked her.

Elwyn laughed. "Right. Anywho, what do you need, Donovan?"

"I need to know more about a kid named Benji Henderson from Ruidoso. The doc seems very close to him."

"Oh, okay. Beeeenjiiii Hennnnderrrrson," she said as she wrote the name down. "What else?"

"Find out about his family, too. If they went on vacation or something. The doc kept talking about the cabin and how it looked abandoned, but it looked fine to me."

"Cabin. Got it."

"Oh, yeah, and there's a dead body on the front porch." When his uninvited guests openly gaped at him, he felt the need to defend himself. "What? I told you, the woman was already dead. Though I may have broken her neck postmortem. Still, there's a funeral home out there somewhere with a missing elderly woman wearing overalls."

Marika frowned at him. "Who buries someone in overalls?"

"Right? I don't smell like embalming fluid, do I?"

"Ew," Elwyn said into the phone.

"I have one more question, Teacup."

"Why you?" she said matter-of-factly.

"Why me?" he confirmed.

"Because I knew you wouldn't let anything happen to her."

"What makes you say that?"

"Because you're in love with her."

He hesitated and then repeated his question. "What makes you say that?"

"Because you never take your eyes off her when she comes to the compound, unless she's looking at you, of course. That's when you pretend you don't know she exists."

"I do no such thing."

"You're such a guy," she said, her attitude shining through.

He tried not to chuckle. Failed. "I guess I am."

"Okay, gotta go learn stuff, even though I could teach my history teacher a thing or two."

"Elwyn," Swopes said, a warning tone in his voice. "We talked about this."

"I know, I know. By the way, I'm sending help in case you're attacked again, Donovan."

"Yeah?"

"Artemis has been dying to see you."

Artemis, a Rottweiler with the heart of a gladiator, had been his dog before an asshole who had the audacity to call himself a human being poisoned her. The man was lucky he still had the ability to breathe without medical intervention. After she passed, she'd become Charley's guardian somehow—and now Elwyn's. He was oddly proud of her. He'd raised her from a pup and, from what he'd been told, she could rip a demon to shreds in seconds flat. He teared up every time he thought about it.

"Artemis speaks English now?" he asked her.

"No, but every time you come to the main house, she runs circles around you and whines. She wants your attention so bad."

That realization was a little more than he could handle at the moment. He ignored the tightening in his chest. "I would rather she stay with you. You get into way more trouble than I do."

"Do not."

"She should stick by your side until we know what this thing is."

"You're forgetting I also have twelve hellhounds guarding me night and day."

"True."

"Speaking of which, I'm also sending you King Henry VIII. He and Artemis make a great team."

"Didn't he die?"

"Not *that* King Henry VIII. The hellhound, King Henry VIII."

Donovan sat up. The pain that shot through his body was like a chainsaw ripping him to shreds. "You're sending me a hellhound?"

"He's very sweet."

"You're sending me a hellhound named after a British monarch who beheaded people for breakfast?"

"He's the most regal of them all. And the chunkiest. I think he gets the most demons."

Donovan was almost sorry he'd asked as he tried to ease back onto the bed without creating any undue pain. It didn't work.

Once he'd settled, Swopes handed him two pills and a glass of water. He didn't question it. He would've taken hashish laced with PCP at that point.

"You said you can find the doc?" he asked.

He swallowed the pills and then gestured toward his phone. "I installed an app on her cell so I could track her."

"Isn't that illegal?" Marika asked.

"It most certainly is."

Swopes handed him his smartphone. "So, where is she now?"

He opened the app and zoomed out of her location. "She's heading east. I can catch up when she stops for the night."

"You mean *if* she stops for the night."

"Right." He could have a harder time catching her than he'd hoped. She had a lengthy head start. Trying not to be bitter about that fact, he swung his legs over the side of the bed, wincing with every movement.

Marika sounded worried. "How are you going to drive like that?"

"Very carefully." He winked at her and then looked up at Swopes. "I'm gonna need your shirt."

"The fuck you are."

Chapter Seven

Every warning label has an awesome backstory.
—True fact

He was back. Kursch was back. She never felt him enter her mind. Maybe he didn't have to. Maybe he was just as much a part of Zhou as the human Sia was. The land stretched out before her looked as if it had just been hit by a series of Scud missiles. Smoke bellowed from cars abandoned on the highway. Fires raged all around her. Bodies in the dozens lay strewn across the landscape.

No longer able to trust her mind, Sia had no choice but to pull over. She'd hoped to drive all night, but if she started swerving to miss cars and bodies, she would wreck and likely hurt someone in the process.

She pulled onto the shoulder and shook her head, trying to kick Kursch out of it. It worked. The world sprang back to rolling hills sprinkled with yellow grasses and desert foliage. He'd entered her mind. Did that mean he could locate her? That he could kill her?

Her phone rang. She squinted past the pain of a piercing headache to focus on the screen. *Donovan St. James.* Barbed wire cinched around her heart when she rejected the call and blocked his number. After years of wanting him to notice her, he finally had, but not in the way she'd dreamed. He'd only watched over her on orders from his charge.

And now he would be mad that she'd blocked his number. He had a right to be. He'd risked his life to save her, and she'd left him incapacitated and bleeding in a cheap motel room. Not only that, she'd drugged him. If they'd ever had a chance before, she was certain that ship had sailed.

A voice popped into her head. *Sia?*

Benji? She gasped aloud, then tried to calm herself. This could be another trick. But when he sent her another message, she began to think it was really him. *Believe nothing.*

I know. He's in my head, too. Are you okay? When she didn't receive a reply, she said again, *Benji?*

Nothing. She'd lost him again. Frustration welded her teeth together, but she had to get off the interstate. She eased back onto the blacktop and searched for the next exit. Hopefully, there would be a hotel or even just a convenience store. She was not above sleeping in her car in a parking lot.

When she exited a few minutes later, the sun was still drifting up the horizon. The off-ramp had no hotels, but there was a small mom-and-pop convenience store with a single gas pump. Since her stomach had decided to sing the song of its people, she went inside.

The tiny shop smelled like hot dogs and motor oil. She could work with that. A staticky country song played over the speakers as she fished a hotdog off the warming rack with a set of plastic tongs. She tucked it into a bun and went in search of mustard. The bottle they had was empty. That was when she saw the first dead body. The clerk behind the counter, a kid in his twenties from the looks of him, lay in a pool of blood.

This wasn't happening. This wasn't real. She dropped the hotdog and shook her head again, but the image stayed put. Backing toward the exit, she looked down a short hall that led to the bathrooms. A tall, thin man in a mask stood there, staring at her, a screwdriver in one hand, a machete in the other. Behind him lay another dead body—an elderly gentleman wearing plaid golf pants.

The killer didn't seem to be in any great hurry as he watched her, standing motionless. She soon understood why. The glass door at her back was locked. She pressed into it, the handle digging into her spine as she tried to force it open.

A blue Subaru pulled up to the door, and she turned to pound on the glass. The couple looked on in horror, and she realized there was yet another body outside. When Sia made eye contact with them, begging for help, their gazes slid past her, and they sped away.

Then she felt him and stilled. The killer stood behind her. His breath stirred the hair at the back of her head. He smelled like motor oil and rotten eggs, but when she looked at the body outside, a middle-aged woman with blond hair and bright pink Crocs, she knew for certain that none of this was real. She would've seen that body.

Or so she thought until she saw the trail of blood behind it. The woman had evidently crawled to the front from the back of the store, weakly lifting a hand to press it to the glass. But clearly she could only hold the position for so long before her hand slipped, leaving streaks of bright red.

Sia knelt and pressed her fingertips to the door. "Is this real?" she asked, just as the machete sliced across her back.

* * * *

She had pulled over, spurring Donovan to drive faster. There were no hotels near where her tracker seemed to sit on the highway between exits. She hadn't slept all night. Maybe she just couldn't go any farther without catching some Zs, but the interstate was no place to do that.

Of course, these apps were not always accurate. He hoped she'd exited earlier and was pulled over on a side road. He tried calling, but she rejected it. Rejected him.

His phone rang, and he picked up, only a little disappointed that it wasn't the doc. "Aren't you supposed to be in class?"

"I am," Teacup whispered. "Kind of. I'm in some kind of file closet."

"Why are you in a file closet?"

"Because I'm supposed to be in class. Duh."

Not one of his finer moments. "What'd you find out?"

"Okay, the Hendersons are visiting relatives in New Hampshire."

"Really? They don't seem like the New Hampshire type."

After a long pause, she asked, "What's the New Hampshire type?"

"That's a great question. What else do you have?"

"Well, their son, Benji, didn't go with them because of football."

"So, he should have been home?"

"I think he's staying with a friend—a fellow football player. I'm not a hundred percent on that front. Either way, there hasn't been anyone admitted to the nearby hospitals fitting his description, and he hasn't been reported missing, so that's good."

"It is."

"But here's the strange part."

Donovan tilted his head in interest.

"Benji Henderson almost died five years ago on the very same day the doc was attacked."

"Really?"

"Yes. He was playing with some friends near a river and fell off a bridge, breaking his neck."

"He survived a broken neck?"

"And a drowning. Apparently, the cold water saved his life. According to the article, he was submerged for almost forty-five minutes before the rescue team got there and dragged him out."

"So, he survived both a broken neck and drowning. What are the odds of that?"

"They called it a miracle. It was in all the local papers and even made the news in Albuquerque and Santa Fe. There are clips on YouTube. I'll send you a couple of links."

"Thanks, Teacup."

"Can I ask you something in case you die while trying to fight this bad guy and I never see you again?"

Her concern was touching. "Sure."

"Why do you call me Teacup?"

He laughed and regretted it instantly. "Because when you were little, you used to drink coffee out of your plastic tea set. You would hold your teacup just so with your pinky jutting out."

"Really?"

"Also, you fell in love with Chip from *Beauty and the Beast.*"

"The teacup! He was so cute."

"You were three."

"And?"

"You drank more coffee than I did."

"Okay."

"And you were already boy-crazy."

"Your point?"

"No point. Just stating some facts." That kid was Charley, through and through.

"Okay, well, don't die if you can help it."

He suppressed a chuckle that would've hurt. "I'll do my best."

"And, Donovan?"

"Yes, Teacup?"

"I'm not a hundred percent on this either, so don't quote me, but

I'm fairly certain I love you more than just about anyone else on the planet." He stilled, her words sucking the breath right out of his already stressed lungs, but before he could reply, she said, "And save the girl," before hanging up.

He stared straight ahead, wondering what he'd ever done in his life to deserve such adoration from the likes of Charley Davidson's daughter. It may have been because he was often the one giving in to her coffee fetish. But his intentions had been in the name of self-preservation. The kid had ADHD like nobody's business. He could hardly keep up. Coffee was the only thing that calmed her down.

He swiped a hand across his mouth, trying to erase the shit-eating grin he now wore. God, he loved her.

He glanced down at his phone. According to the app, the doc's vehicle was stopped about two miles ahead of him. Sure enough, he crested a hill and spotted the red crossover on the right shoulder, haphazardly parked, almost as though she'd rolled into the guardrail. He depressed the gas pedal and made it over in record time.

Normally, he would have jumped out of the truck and run, but that was out of the question at the moment. Instead, he carefully shifted into park, opened his door, and slid down the side of his seat, thanking the maker for factory-installed steps. Each molecule of air he dragged in hurt. Every movement cut through him like glass. But he went as fast as he could, and found the doc slumped against her door.

"Doc!" he yelled, first trying the door and then pounding on the window. "Doc, wake up!"

When she didn't respond, he took out his knife and used the handle to break the back seat driver's side glass. It shattered on his second try as cars and trucks whipped past them.

He reached around, unlocked her door, and carefully opened it, catching her in his arms when she fell against him. "Come on, Doc," he said, patting her pale cheek softly. "You can do it."

She roused at last, but her reaction to him was less than enthusiastic. She scrambled out of his arms, her gaze darting about wildly as she felt her back for... what? When she realized that she wasn't in danger, she sat panting for a solid minute before returning her gaze to his. Then, she lunged at him.

He caught her, pulling her into his arms as she burst into tears and cried on his new-to-him shirt. Despite the pain, he pulled her in as tightly as he could without hurting her. "It's okay, Doc." He gave her some time, simply breathing her in, ignoring the occasional blare of a horn. But the other drivers were right. They needed to get off the interstate. It was too dangerous to be parked there. "Doc?" he said softly.

She lifted her head at last, and the tears shimmering in her eyes made them look even bigger.

"We need to get off the road. Can you follow me to the next exit?"

Fear flashed across her face. "No, there's a killer."

"A killer?" he asked, confused.

She slammed her lids shut, pushing even more tears over her lashes. "No. There's no killer. It was all in my head."

Damn it, was she schizophrenic? He'd had a good friend contract the horrible illness right out of high school. His entire life had been ahead of him, and he'd ended up losing everything.

"How about you just come with me?"

"What?" She seemed to return to the present. "No, it's okay. I can follow you."

"You sure? I can walk back for your car once I get you to safety."

Her expression softened. "No, I'm good. I'll follow you."

He nodded warily and walked back to his truck. Ten minutes later, they sat in his cab at Love's Truck Stop. She'd parked her car, grabbed her bag, and rushed into his passenger's seat as though scared to death that something would reach out and grab her. And he wanted to know why.

"Okay, Doc, what gives?" he asked as she dug through her purse.

"Did you drink the medication I left for you?"

"What was that anyway? It knocked me out."

"I told you, it was liquid Lortab."

"I've had Lortab, and it does not do that."

She pursed her pretty lips at him. "First off, you were exhausted. Second, the moment the pain began to subside, that exhaustion took over, and you were finally able to rest." She took out the bottle and poured some into the cap. "Here."

"Are you sure this won't knock me out?"

"It shouldn't unless you really need it—which you probably do. How are your ribs?"

"Better now," he said, meaning it. Either her presence had somehow lessened the pain, or his endorphins were finally kicking in.

Possibly a little of both. He tipped the cap at his lips, then handed it back to her. "You just walk around with narcotics in your bag?"

"It's for emergencies only."

"Ah. So, what's going on?"

She replaced the bottle, slid her medical kit onto the floorboard, then looked out the window without answering.

"Let me tell you what I do know."

Her gaze dropped to the hands she twisted in her lap.

"You were attacked in an alley five years ago at the exact same time that strange epidemic was going on."

"You and I both know what happened."

"I do. Shade demons had slipped onto this plane and were taking over the bodies of people with mental illnesses, sending them into fits of violence. So, yes, I *do* know what happened. I'm just surprised you do." When she didn't respond, he asked, "Is that what happened? Did one of them attack you?"

"No comment."

"Doc, look. If I'm going to help you—"

"What can you do?" she asked, her defenses rising. She lifted her trembling chin and said, "I was trying to keep you out of this. You're just a human."

"Ouch and... what?" He narrowed his gaze on her. "Does that mean you're not?"

She sucked in a soft breath as though just realizing what she'd said. "No, of course, it doesn't mean that."

"Okay, what about Benji?"

Her head whipped around to him. "What about him?"

"He almost died, as well. On the exact same day *you* almost died, actually."

She lifted a shoulder.

"And you both survived against impossible odds. Don't you find that strange?"

"Not at all. I'm a doctor. I see that kind of thing all the time."

"Did you even go to school with Charley?" he asked, begging her to open up to him. He decided to change tactics. To go for the jugular. "Or was that a lie, too?" He tilted his head and added softly, "Leech."

She stilled, and a fresh pool of tears gathered between her lashes. He was such an ass.

"You're not human, are you? Not entirely."

"You're not acting very human either at the moment."

"Maybe not, but at least I was born with this soul. Where did yours come from?"

She turned away, but he saw a tear escape through her reflection in the window and fought against the sympathy he felt for her. It would do neither of them any good.

"I don't have much time," she said after a long moment of contemplation. "You're right. You need to know in case I don't survive." She turned and faced him to drive her point home. "It will come for Elwyn, and there's nothing you can do to stop it."

Chapter Eight

The real problem with reality is the lack of background music.
—Meme

She no longer had a choice. Sia had to tell the gang that an entity of pure evil had somehow slipped onto the plane and that it would come for their beloved Elwyn. Now that Sia knew for certain that Kursch was responsible for the things that were happening, she had an obligation to report him. The soul eater was a master manipulator of the mind, and they needed to know what he was capable of.

Then again, was this even real? Had Donovan really woken her? Or was this all a part of Kursch's sick games?

There had been no escaping him in the void. Here, however, there seemed to be obstacles and interferences. How else would she have awakened from her latest horror fest? And why had Kursch left that corpse's body when Donovan broke its neck? The woman was already dead. What did a broken neck matter?

Was it Donovan? Both times, he'd emitted an extreme amount of emotion. The first was when Kursch was about to shoot her. The second when he thought she might be hurt or dying in her car. Was that it? Was it human emotion? Or was it...?

She dropped her gaze and noticed something she hadn't paid much attention to before. Well, she *had*, actually. Donovan always wore several bracelets on his wrists. For reasons she couldn't fathom, she found that fact very sexy. But one of them was black with Indigenous symbols on it.

She reached out and touched it. He let her, despite the disgust he must've felt. "Is that iron?"

He twisted it around to give her a better view. "It is."

She covered her mouth with both hands in astonishment. When Donovan touched the woman with his bracelet, Kursch had fled. And when he touched Sia with the same bracelet, Kursch's presence in her mind had dissipated. They had speculated that iron would hurt the soul eater—or, well, Charley had speculated. She'd given them the answer to defeating Kursch years ago, and they never knew.

Sia grabbed her phone and texted Benji. *We were right. Iron is his kryptonite. Tell the others.*

"Now that we've gotten past the show-and-tell portion of our program, care to elaborate on what exactly is coming for the teacup?"

She no longer cared what Donovan thought about her. He may hate her. He may find her disgusting, but her elation could not be contained. She lunged forward and threw her arms around his neck yet again.

He froze for a long moment before relaxing and sliding his large hands around her waist. The warmth of them trailed across her stomach and over her back, and she sank against him.

She tried not to cry. It was surely getting old. But he had quite possibly saved them all. Or, at the very least, saved Elwyn since Sia would likely die trying to defeat Kursch. "Iron," she said against his neck. "Tell everyone that Kursch can be stopped with iron."

"Iron. Got it. Is Kursch your ex or something?"

A bubble of laughter burst out of her. She'd been so scared for so long, but now there was a chance. Not, like, a huge one, but... She sank back and lowered her gaze. "You were right. I'm not entirely human. But I'm not a demon either," she rushed to add.

He chewed on his lower lip, the act so sexy she was certain her human body ovulated. Then he asked softly, "What *are* you?"

"I'm kind of like what you would consider a ghost. Only on my world—one that Kursch destroyed, by the way—certain plant life had souls, as well. Just like humans do. We worked synergistically with the foliage we inhabited. We are basically the spiritual remnants of a type of plant that poisons its enemies using an irresistible scent."

He eased back to get a better look at her. "Is that why you smell so good?"

She offered a sheepish shrug. "It's possible."

"Wait, can it kill me?"

She laughed. "I don't think so. Not directly, anyway."

He shook his head as though astonished. "Tell me more."

"Are you sure?"

"One hundred percent."

"Okay, well, we were elementals living on a very hostile but starkly beautiful planet. We were known to be very powerful, so Kursch ravaged our world, rounded us up, and sent us into a void where he could feed off our energy for eons." She glanced up to assess Donovan's reaction. When his expression remained neutral, she continued. "We languished in the void for so long, we forgot anything else. Until a certain god named Elle-Rhyn-Ahleethia showed up on our doorstep." Sia grinned at him. "You know her as Charley Davidson."

He gaped at her. "You're from Marmalade?"

She laughed. "How did you know she named it that? It was so funny because we didn't know what it meant until we followed her here. It's quite yummy."

"Did all of your kind escape?"

"No." A wave of sadness swept over her. "When she was sent back, only a few of us were lucky enough to make it through before the portal closed. But she's the one who opened our eyes. Who showed us what Kursch was doing to us. Feeding off us. Manipulating our minds."

"That's why you're seeing things that aren't there."

"Yes. But it seems the iron in your bracelet somehow scares him off. Or maybe it hurts him. Charley told us it would. I don't know how she knew, but she told us iron was his weakness. That we could use it to fight him. To possibly escape the void."

"Did she happen to mention where to find said iron, what with you being in a void and all?

"We didn't get that far, but I think she had a plan."

"I'm sure she did. She's pretty amazing."

"She is."

"About this body," he said, swinging back around to the elephant in the room.

"The doctor was attacked. But not by a possessed like you think."

He reached over and took her hand as though fascinated with her fingers. He ran the tips of his over the length of hers. It sent waves of pleasure spiraling through her body. "Then who attacked her?"

She cleared her throat and tried to ignore what he was doing to her. "Her ex."

His gaze shot to hers.

"Don't worry," she continued. "He's dead."

"She killed him?"

"No. But she fought back for all she was worth. She inflicted a lot of damage, but he was like a raging bull, striking blindly because she dared to reject him. He was still attacking her when she died. When I took possession, for lack of a better phrase."

"And you killed him?"

"I did. Just barely. I was able to wrest control of the knife and, having just acquired an encyclopedic knowledge of human anatomy, knew exactly where to stab him to inflict the most damage."

"There wasn't anything about him in the articles about her death."

"There wouldn't have been. He wasn't found with her. He ran afterward and managed to put several blocks between them. Since they'd barely dated and had never gone public—she'd picked up on the red flags left and right early in their relationship—the cops never connected the two." She lowered her head. "It was blind luck that I found her when I did. That I was able to retaliate for her. I healed her body just enough to make survival plausible, then waited for help to arrive."

He turned to look out his window. "How do you know she picked up red flags?"

"I have all of her memories. It's how I can practice medicine. I know everything she did."

"So, you just took up where she left off?"

"I did." She drew in a shaky breath. "And now you know. I have to find Benji, but I need a favor."

He turned back to her.

"Can I borrow your bracelet? I think it will keep Kursch out of my head long enough for us to come up with a plan. I'm hoping we can kill him before he catches wind of Elwyn."

"How do you know he hasn't already?"

"We don't. All the more reason to kill him if we can."

He nodded in thought, a frown lining his impossibly handsome face. Sia understood. It was a lot to take in, even for someone with Donovan's experience. His doubt crystal-clear, he asked, "And you and this high school kid are gonna save the day?"

"Along with the others, if they're still alive. If not, I'll do it alone. I can't let him find the girl destined to save humanity. I've grown fond of it."

"So, you're going to sacrifice yourself for the teacup?"

She deadpanned him. "Like you wouldn't do the same."

"Of course, I would. Okay." He clapped his hands together and rubbed them as though preparing to do a magic trick. "I'm in."

"In?"

"In."

"Wait." She shifted in her seat. "No. There's no in. There's just me and possibly Benji and, well, I don't know about the others. We lost contact. But that's it. You don't get to be in."

"Right, because I'm only human."

She winced. "Sorry about that. But this isn't your fight."

"If it involves the teacup," he said with a glare, "it is absolutely my fight."

A sensuality laced up her spine, stealing the breath from her lungs. His masculine face showed a determination she didn't dare question. His sharp jaw covered in that scruff that somehow had the power to transform her legs to jelly. The sprinkling of gray at his temples. The long lashes, and his rich, blue irises that sometimes sparkled from underneath. He was so darkly handsome. So devastatingly rugged. She could get used to being a human if she got to look at that every day.

"You know I only called you a leech to piss you off."

She huffed out a soft laugh. "It's okay. You're right."

"No, I'm not. I wanted the truth. Now, I have it. You're ethereal, Doc. A beautiful soul wrapped in a beautiful body."

"You think I'm beautiful?"

"Very."

"And you think this body is beautiful?"

"I do," he said, humor sparkling in his eyes.

He took a sip of bottled water right as she asked, "Would you like it?" Then he coughed for the next five minutes, and she wanted to be humiliated. She tried to be, but she couldn't quite manage it. She wanted him, and there was no time like the hours leading up to one's certain death to get the juices flowing. The heart racing. The desperation skyrocketing. It was now or never, and she knew it. "I'm sorry," she said as he wiped his mouth on the bottom of his dark gray T-shirt. "Would you like a tissue?" She grabbed her bag and began combing through the contents.

"It's okay. This isn't my shirt," he said, pressing the shirt tail to his mouth like a kid.

Too bad. It showed off his sinuous forearms and thick biceps perfectly. But it was the abs he'd just flashed that undid her.

"Should we, um, do you want to get a hotel room?" Was he actually nervous? Because butterflies were currently dive-bombing the lining of her stomach. Still, she figured him for a pro. He certainly looked the part.

"Well," she said, looking around, "your windows are pretty tinted. And you have that nifty sun shade for your windshield."

"Wait. Here?"

She took a deep breath to muster her courage and crawled over the console to straddle him.

His surprise only lasted a moment. He reached down and adjusted the seat so the steering wheel was no longer cupping her butt. Instead, his hands were.

She leaned forward and pressed her mouth to his. Yep. That same delicious tension coiled low in her abdomen just like the last two times she'd kissed him. The sensation intensified when he slid his tongue along her lower lip, and a soft whimper escaped before she could stop it. Embarrassed, she pulled back and dropped her gaze. "By the way," she said, a warmth spreading over her face, "I'm a virgin."

* * * *

Donovan froze. He held her against him until he could collect his thoughts. It took a while. After staring at her for a solid sixty seconds, he asked, "You're a what?" just to confirm.

Her huge eyes found his again, a stunning mixture of caramel and deeper browns with flecks of sea-foam green sprinkled throughout. "I mean, this body isn't, but I am. I've never... you know."

"Ah, got it." That made more sense. Not that a beautiful, successful woman couldn't be a virgin. The odds were definitely against it, though. "So, I'll be your first," he said matter-of-factly. No pressure.

"Technically. I mean, I know what to do. Technically. I've just never actually put that knowledge to the test."

"Is this a test?" he asked, grinning at her. She seemed more nervous than he was. "Tests were never my strong point in school."

"What was?"

"Girls, mostly."

She giggled. There was no other word for it. A short, soft bubble of laughter escaped her, and he found her even more enchanting because of it. "Why aren't I surprised?" she asked.

"I can't imagine. But first things first." He slipped the metal bracelet off, pushed the two ends together to close the circle, and slid it onto her much slenderer wrist. "It's still too big." He went to take it back but she snatched her hand away.

"It's perfect." She lifted it to study as though examining a cluster of diamonds. "But you really shouldn't have." When he only grinned at her, she added, "I feel like I'm leaving you vulnerable by taking this."

"He's not after me. I'll be fine."

She dropped her wrist and her gaze. "Should we start then?"

He lifted a brow. "Start?"

"Yeah, you know. It."

"Ah." He tried not to smile. He failed. This was going to be fun. "Where do you suggest we begin?"

"Oh." Her eyes rounded as she thought about his question much more intently than he'd imagined she would. "Right. Well, music seems to be important."

"Music." He nodded and fought that errant grin again. The fucker. "What would you suggest?"

"I'm not sure." She pressed her mouth to one side as she considered it. "Maybe something bow-chicka-wow-ish?"

He had to refocus every ounce of strength in his body to keep from laughing. To hide his face, he leaned past her to turn on the radio. "Let's just see what's available."

"Right. Good idea."

After a quick search, something appropriately smooth came on.

"Oh, Rihanna!" she said, clapping softly. Then, as though embarrassed, she added, "This is a good song."

"I'll take your word for it. What next?"

"Hmmm." She tapped her chin with an index finger. "Well, I don't want to seem forward—"

"Of course, not."

"—but you should probably take off your shirt."

"Just me?"

She glanced down at her zippered hoodie. "Good point. I mean, it's only fair, right?"

"Fair is fair."

"Fair is definitely fair." She started to unzip the hoodie but stopped when he didn't move to do the same.

When she pointed her chin at the T-shirt, he reached for the back of the collar and lifted it over his head. He could've sworn he heard a soft gasp, but he wasn't sure.

He tossed Swopes' tee onto the passenger's seat, and she slowly lowered the zipper on her hoodie without taking her eyes off his chest. He suddenly worried that his tattoos would turn her off. She didn't seem to be bothered, but there was an entire demographic that found them appalling. Which was probably a big part of the reason he'd gotten them in the first place. Nothing like presenting himself as a hellraiser to keep the puritans at bay. He was a walking defense mechanism. Would she see through him? Did he care?

With a jolt of surprise, he realized that he did. But why? He'd never cared. Then again, he'd never met anyone like the doc. And that was before he knew what she was. Most of the women he'd taken to his bed had practically begged him to do so. He'd never hit on a woman in his life. He'd never had to. But the doc was different. He could see himself begging for her attention. Willingly. Gladly. Desperately.

When she literally separated one tooth of the zipper at a time, her movements painstakingly slow, he couldn't take it any longer. He took the zipper out of her hands, slid it all the way down, and peeled the jacket off her shoulders.

Her powerful scent engulfed him. Exotic and sweet, it surrounded, saturated, and stirred, pumping blood into his cock. When she started on the buttons of her white blouse, he didn't have it in him to wait. Praying the garment didn't cost more than his Harley, he took the edges and ripped it open. Her breasts, held by the barest hint of a lace bra, spilled forth, and for a moment, he was mesmerized. Until his gaze dropped to her stomach. To the side of her ribs. To her right shoulder.

It was like someone threw a bucket of ice water on him. No, not ice water. Boiling honey. When she went to cover her midsection with her arms, he didn't let her. He took hold of her wrists and locked them behind her back for a better look.

Scars of every size and shape adorned her beautiful body, and his blood turned bitingly cold. He didn't realize how much so until she winced and jerked her hands out of his grip.

"I'm sorry," he said, but it was too late. He'd ruined the mood. He bit back a curse when she pulled her shirt together and climbed off his lap.

Chapter Nine

Know thy lane and
stay the fuck in it.
—Charley 1:12

Sia could hardly blame Donovan for being shocked. For finding this body unattractive. For finding *her* unattractive. She pulled the shirt together, her shoulders inching up as she tried to climb out of his lap.

He stayed her with two large hands on her shoulders.

She fought a sting at the backs of her eyes but couldn't look at him. Humiliation tore through her like a wildfire, hot and all-consuming. She'd been too brazen, too bold when she had no right to be. He was a god compared to her, and she was barely even human.

"It's okay," she said, trying to wiggle out of his embrace. "We don't have to do anything."

"We'll get to that. Are you sure he's dead?" he asked, his voice hoarse and yet razor-sharp.

She frowned. "Who?"

"The man who did this to you."

She huffed out a laugh. "You forget, he didn't do this to me. He did it to Dr. Lucia Mirabal."

"You said he was still attacking when you entered her body. Do you still have the memories of what he did?" he asked, his eyes glittering with anger. "Do you remember the knife cutting into this gorgeous flesh?"

"I do," she admitted. "Like it happened yesterday."

"Then he did it to you."

"No, Donovan. He didn't. What that woman went through..."

"And you, in turn. Don't downplay that."

She gave up and answered his question. "Yes, I'm sure he's dead." She tried to climb out of his lap again, but he held her fast.

"We were in the middle of something."

"It's okay. Really. I need to go anyway." But his hands tightened around her upper arms, his thumbs rubbing over the material of her blouse like cat tails, the movement comforting.

"Do you think the scars have somehow changed my feelings toward you?"

"Why wouldn't they?"

"Did my tattoos change your feelings toward me?"

That was a good question. They did, in fact. The first time she'd treated him. How could she explain it? "In a way, yes." She felt him tense beneath her, so she quickly explained. "They made you even more alluring. More forbidden."

His sapphire irises glittered with what she hoped was interest. "And your scars do that for me."

"How?" she asked, her tone filled with the doubt she felt to the depths of her soul.

"They show what a fighter she was. What a survivor you are. They are as beautiful and foreboding as you are, and I would very much like to pick up where we left off."

She lifted a shoulder and examined the unpolished nails on her right hand. "I guess we can. This body has strong feelings for you."

"Only the body?" he asked, his voice soft with humor.

"I feel stupid, though. I know what to do, but I'm doing it all wrong."

He captured her chin. "Trust me, gorgeous, you are doing nothing wrong."

"Really?"

"Really."

"If I do something stupid, you'll tell me?"

He raised three fingers. "Swear."

"Were you even a Boy Scout?"

"Of course. I would never betray the code."

She narrowed her eyes on him and said, "So, if I do this..." Right before she leaned forward and pressed her mouth to his, but only for a second.

He tilted his head as though his interest had been piqued. "That's certainly a good start."

She nodded. "How about this?" She ran a hand down his chest, across his stomach, and over his rib cage.

His muscles flexed under her touch, the ridges that covered his lean midsection fascinating her. "That works, too."

"What about this?" She shrugged the shirt off her shoulders and began unfastening her jeans, her fingers shaking more than she would have liked. This whole seduction thing was proving far more complex than she'd thought. Even though she was the actor, and he the act-ee, she felt like she was the one being seduced every time he gazed at her, his narrowed lids making his irises glisten all the more.

He watched her hands with something similar to hunger, and she noticed his chest rising and falling a bit quicker than it had before. That fact delighted her.

She managed to unfasten the button and get the zipper halfway down, but the restricted space was becoming a problem. "Hold on," she said before scooting her butt over the console and reclining on the passenger-side seat. Once there, she shimmied the jeans over her hips and down her legs, only to realize she was wearing boots. "Keep holding on. I'm still on this step. Withhold judgment."

"Not. A. Problem."

She eased into a crunch to peer at him from over her knees. Or one knee. The other leg was in the air as she tried to get the boot off. Even so, he studied her, his expression part tax assessor and part wolf. Whatever he was thinking, she liked it. The muscles in his jaw bunched as he watched her work, and his tongue slid out to lick his top lip.

When she finally got the damned boot off, she kicked off the jeans, but he slid a finger into her powder-blue panties, the backs of his fingers brushing over her clit in the process, spiking something wonderful deep inside her.

"These, too."

"Okay." She peeled off the lingerie and sat up, her breaths now coming in short bursts. But he was gone. "Donovan?" she asked just as the back door opened.

He climbed into the back seat and said softly, "Come here."

The butterflies in her stomach took up strategic positions and attacked with a bloodthirsty kind of vigor. She filled her lungs then stood to scale the seat. Once she was halfway, he helped her, lifting her over the backrests and onto his lap, where she once again straddled him. She settled onto him, not missing the outline of his cock between his legs.

He pushed a stray lock of hair back from her face and pulled her down until her mouth was on his again. He parted her lips with his tongue, and while that felt wonderful, his fingers sliding over her clit felt even better. She stiffened and grabbed his wrist. Not because she didn't like it, but because she liked it too much.

"It's okay," he said at her mouth as though he knew exactly what she was thinking. Maybe he did. She didn't care in the least. One arm slid around her shoulders and pulled her closer as though to hold her still as he worked. "Spread your legs farther."

She realized she'd clamped her legs against his as though trying to close them. She tried to relax, but the waves of pleasure pulsing through her wouldn't allow it.

He pulled her to him until his mouth was at her ear. "I'm going to have you for dinner now."

"What?" she asked, her voice a breathy ghost of what it had been only minutes earlier. But she understood when he put his arms under her knees, scooted down a bit, and lifted her until her clit was at his mouth.

She gasped aloud and grabbed handfuls of his hair. His tongue brushed softly between the folds of her core, teasing her clit with delicious precision. Her muscles contracted in response, and she felt warmth pool in her abdomen. A sharp tightness coiled deep inside.

Without breaking contact, he twisted and laid her on the seat, his thick arms easily handling her weight. She rose onto her shoulder blades anyway, jutting her hips heavenward, worried he would stop. To keep him locked to her, she curled handfuls of hair into her fists, and while she couldn't be certain, he may have laughed. But it was worth it. Any embarrassment she may suffer later was nothing compared to what this man was doing with his tongue.

He combined swirls with soft suckling and occasional kisses. But the fingers sliding into her warmth were her undoing. The pressure in her abdomen built to a piercing release of pleasure. It spilled into her in wave after succulent wave. She bucked off the seat as he pushed his fingers into her in time with her climax.

Then he eased on top of her and trailed hot kisses up her neck and across her jaw until he captured her mouth with his. As she soared onto another plane of existence, he slid into her in one smooth thrust. The movement caught her off guard. She clamped around him as his thickness sent her spiraling a second time.

He pushed into her slowly at first, but she wanted more. And she wanted it faster. She lifted her hips off the seat again and grasped his rounded buttocks to force him deeper, glad that the doctor's body was not as virginal as she.

"Doc," he said, his voice deep and breathy, but that was all he said before he climaxed himself.

It was only fair. She was going on her third peak, the sensations washing over her like heroin mixed with highly volatile explosives. She held her breath, hoping for one more second of ecstasy, one more moment of pleasure. When Donovan shuddered and groaned, his expression part euphoria and part agony, she got it. His release lengthened hers, and she watched his gorgeous face tense and relax when he came down.

He started to collapse onto her but stopped himself, so she pulled him down and wrapped her arms and legs around him in a vise grip as they panted in rhythm.

"On a scale of one to ten?" she asked after a few minutes, and he laughed, a deep, husky thing that almost sent her over the edge again. "Soooo, maybe a nine-point-three-eight-five?" When he only kissed her neck, sending spirals of pleasure down her spine, she decided for herself. "It was a nine-point-three-eight-five."

* * * *

Sia had never felt anything like that in her life. She'd read all about orgasms in both nonfiction and fiction books, but the reality was so much better. So much sharper. So much more earth-shatteringly intense.

She kissed Donovan softly on the mouth and then left him snoozing in the back seat of his truck to get a fresh set of clothes from her car. Unable to stop herself, she gazed lovingly at the bracelet he'd insisted she wear until they could get her one that fit her wrist better. For now, she would cherish this one.

After crawling into the back seat, she opened her suitcase and sought out a fresh set of clothes. They planned to drive straight through to North Carolina. Donovan had agreed to help her find her friends, and one of them was inhabiting a pastry chef in Asheville named Pamela Dubois. But they would have to find some showers soon—one of the perks of living on this plane. She tugged on her shoes and grabbed the iron dagger. Since Donovan had insisted she take his bracelet, he would carry the dagger in his belt. Have it at the ready. Just as she started to head back to his truck, Benji's voice popped into her head.

Sia, wait.

Benji! she fairly shouted to him. When he didn't answer, she concentrated hard, trying to get him back. *Where are you? Are you okay? Wait for what?*

I'm sorry. He's just too powerful, and I can't live with that kind of terror.

What are you talking about?

I'm sorry.

She whirled around, glancing out of the windows, trying to find something he would have to apologize for. That was when she saw him. The tall, masked man from her vision stood between her car and Donovan's truck, staring at her, his head angled slightly. Only instead of a machete, he carried a gas can in one hand and a lit match in the other.

She scrambled to get out of her car, but the man dropped the match before she could manage it. Panic took hold, and she bolted out the door, falling forward onto the asphalt and scraping her palms on the gravel. She twisted around to watch her car go up in flames, only the trail of fire went the other direction.

"Donovan?" she said softly. A microsecond later, the truck exploded with a deafening bang.

A blast of heat washed over her, followed by raining metallic debris. Her instincts should have taken hold. She should have huddled against the explosion. Protected her head and body the best she could, but she couldn't tear her gaze from the fire billowing thirty feet into the air.

"Donovan?" she whispered again before stumbling toward the truck. The heat refused to let her get very close, and the next few minutes played out like a slow-motion movie.

People circled the truck from a safe distance, yelling at her to get back. But they sounded like they were underwater, their warnings nothing more than muffled pleas.

Why was she seeing this? She was wearing the iron bracelet.

Kursch shouldn't have been able to get into her head. So why was she seeing this?

I'm sorry.

She tried again to get closer, but the wall of heat held her back as though it were made of molten steel. So, she walked around to the driver's side, looking in the back seat for Donovan. Maybe he'd gotten out. Perhaps he'd gone inside the truck stop for a restroom break or for snacks.

She turned and searched for him in the crowd, but he wasn't there.

"There was someone inside!" a woman shouted, and screams and chatter followed her statement. But Sia didn't see anyone. No. He wasn't in there. That woman was wrong.

Sirens blared in the distance as people rushed to move their vehicles lest they go up in flames, as well, but Sia couldn't move. She stared into the fire until her eyes dried out from her efforts.

"Donovan?" she whispered yet again, as though he would be able to hear her even if he wasn't in the truck.

Finally, one man braved the heat and rushed forward to pull her back. She fought him tooth and nail, but he held firm until he got her far enough away from the truck for another onlooker to help wrestle her to the ground. "If someone was in there, they're gone, sweetheart," a woman said to her. "You have to stay back."

This wasn't happening. She looked at her wrist to make sure the bracelet was still there. It was. This couldn't be real. This was just another of Kursch's warped visions.

Then she saw him. The tall man, only he no longer wore the mask. He stood staring at her from the other side of the truck, the flames distorting his elongated face. But there was no mistaking that smile for anything other than the wicked thing it was. Even the fact that his mouth was partially decomposed, exposing his teeth on one side.

She heard them before she saw them. The man and woman still held onto her arms, keeping her locked to the ground as first responders rushed into the lot. But she could hear their growls, low and guttural, even over the sirens. One came up on her left and the other on her right. The thin man's smile faltered when he saw them, but he quickly locked it back into place.

Sia smiled at him and whispered, "Kill."

They bolted forward, the hellhound and the Rottweiler taking off after the man like rockets. He stumbled back and tried to run, but they were on him in an instant. His screams mingled with the vicious sounds of their growls as they dragged the entity out of the body he'd stolen and proceeded to rip it to shreds.

While she didn't doubt for a second that their love bites hurt, she did doubt their ability to kill him. He'd been feeding off the energy of the ka-zhouah for eons. It would take more than a good dismembering to take him out.

She rose to her feet, shaking off the strangers' holds, and walked toward the fight. The human's body lay crumpled on the ground, and the soul eater lay in pieces all around it. The dogs were still snarling and ripping when Sia found what she was looking for. The dark center. The heart of the entity known as Kursch.

The dogs stopped to watch her. King Henry growled whenever a piece moved, knowing it would try to reassemble itself. Artemis bounded up to Sia, something that resembled an arm hanging out of her mouth.

"Good girl," Sia said, patting the adorable Rottweiler on the head. Then she looked at Henry, pointed at the dark center, and said, "Fetch."

Firefighters were now spraying down the truck, but she couldn't think about that right now. She couldn't think about what she'd lost between one second and the next.

Henry gathered the dark center into his mouth, trotted over, and dropped it at her feet.

She knelt and took the iron dagger out of the back of her pants.

No, Kursch said to her a microsecond before she lifted the knife high into the air and plunged it into the core that made him what he was. It didn't melt like she'd hoped. Or turn to dust. Or even explode. It just... disappeared, taking the weight she'd felt on her shoulders for the entire five years she'd been on this plane with it.

But she stayed glued to the spot. Unable to move. Unwilling to. What happened when you were finally able to live freely but no longer wanted to?

Artemis, upset that her arm had disappeared, licked Sia's face, but she only stared at the place where the dark center had been. She felt the heat of the truck at her back. The cool sprinkles of water that bounced off it. The searing scent of burning gasoline and plastics.

I'm so sorry.

She felt Benji beside her but didn't bother to look.

He made me lure you to my house. Then he made me contact you. He got a lock on your location every time I did, but he kept losing it.

"It was the iron from Donovan's bracelet," she said aloud rather than mentally. He didn't need in her thoughts anymore.

Yes. First, it was because you were in the haven, so he forced me to lure you out from under it. Then, yes, it was the bracelet. I'm so sorry, Zhou.

"It's not your fault," she said, her voice monotone. "Kursch had a way of slowly driving us all insane and then forcing us to tip him for giving us a ride."

She felt rather than saw Benji sit beside her.

We all have to find new bodies—everyone but you. But we're free, Sia.

"I'm so sorry for your human family. I know how much they loved you and how much you grew to love them."

He didn't say anything for a long while as first responders rushed around her. Every so often, one would ask if she was injured. She only shook her head, and they went about their business.

They'll find his body soon, Benji said, speaking about his human's physical form. *I'm sorry for them, too.*

"What will you do now?"

I'm thinking about saving that man you fell in love with.

Hope rose inside her until she realized what he meant. He would inhabit Donovan's body. "Don't you dare. It won't be the same."

He's still alive.

It took a moment for his words to sink in. She turned to him and looked at the incorporeal being sitting beside her. He shone a soft blue, as all of them did in their spiritual forms.

His heartbeat is faint, but his soul is still intact. At least, for the moment.

She whirled around and looked at the smoking, water-drenched pickup. He was right. She felt the soft, slow beat of Donovan's heart. Felt the warm rush of his soul. But he could die any moment.

Stumbling to her feet, she rushed forward until a long, muscular arm wrapped around her and pulled her back into the crowd. She fought it, trying to get to Donovan, but a woman's voice stopped her in her tracks.

"If it isn't Mocha Cappuccino."

Sia twisted around until none other than the unsinkable Charley Davidson came into view. She stood with her arms crossed over her chest. Her long, chestnut hair hung over her shoulders, and her gold eyes shimmered with the mischief Sia remembered so fondly from their century together in the void.

"You know who I am?"

"How could I forget? We were BFFs for, like, a hundred years."

"Well, technically seventy, as you were too snooty to mingle with the common folk for the first thirty."

Charley laughed and pulled Sia out of her husband's arms and into hers. "I think you have that backward," she said. "I had no idea you guys made it onto the plane."

"Well, you were a little busy stopping an apocalypse and protecting the kid destined to save humanity and all. She's incredible, by the way. And so much like you, it's scary."

Charley flashed her a nuclear smile and gestured toward the tall glass of water that was her husband. "And the man who just accosted you is—"

"Reyes Farrow," Sia said, holding out her hand. "Welcome back to Earth."

His hand swallowed hers. "I've heard a lot about you."

"Yeah, Marmalade was one giant slumber party."

"Oh," Charley said, "remember that time we punked Salted Caramel Macchiato, and he didn't talk to us for like ten years?"

Sia laughed softly, but Reyes just shook his head. "Thank you for taking care of Team Beep while we were gone."

"Please, it's been my pleasure." She turned back to the truck and struggled to talk with a lump in her throat. "But I think I might have to move on now."

"There's still time," Charley said, but she directed it at Benji.

"He can't, Charley," she said. "If he inhabits an—"

"—occupied host," Charley interrupted, "the host will retain control. He knows what will happen."

That was true. They all did. It was a lesson they learned early on. The host had to have left the building first. Otherwise, the soul inhabiting the body at the time a ka-zhouah entered would still be in control. The ka-zhouah would only be a passenger, but their auras were so powerful, it would still be able to heal the host.

"But he will still be there," Charley added.

I can heal him, Benji said.

"And how would we explain that?"

Do we care? he asked. *Are we caring about that now?*

"Benji, why would you even consider this?"

Because we'll still be together. She felt his essence slide into her fingers. They had been friends for so long, and she loved him dearly. But this was a big ask.

Her chin quivered as she fought the urge to hope. The desire to fall to her knees and beg him to save Donovan. But before she could say anything, before she could do the unthinkable and ask her best friend to sacrifice himself for the love of her life, he was gone.

She gasped and then turned slowly toward the truck.

"Oh, my God. He's alive!" someone shouted.

Emergency personnel rushed to get the back door open, and Donovan St. James unfolded out of the cab, water dripping off him, smoke curling over his broad shoulders, and nary a mark on him. Sia's knees almost gave way beneath her. Had Benji healed him that quickly? Or maybe the fire had yet to spread to the inside of the cab before being doused in water?

Ignoring the EMT trying to put a blanket over his shoulders, he walked up to her, did the hair thing, and pulled her into his arms.

"Are you still Donovan?"

The grin he wore answered for her, but his reply was worth the second affirmation. "I am. Unless you want me to be Captain America. I look fantastic in a leotard." He turned to Charley and Reyes. "Aren't you guys supposed to be running my bar?"

"We handed the reins over to Beep for a few days," Charley said. "She'll do great."

"Like that poor kid hasn't been through enough. Holy fuck, is that what I think it is?"

Sia turned and saw the hellhound sniffing Charley's boots as she rubbed his ears. "That's King Henry VIII," she said.

"That is so much scarier than I thought it would be. I'm not sure seeing into the supernatural realm will be worth it."

Sia pointed to his left. "You might be surprised."

Artemis ran up to them, her stubby little tail wagging a thousand miles an hour.

He knelt to her and buried his face in her fur. "Okay, this is cool."

"That's what I thought," Sia said.

He wrapped an arm around her leg, keeping her close as he got reacquainted with the dog that'd stolen his heart. After a few moments, he looked up at Sia and said, "We should probably get to know each other better first, but do you want to get married next week?"

She knelt next to him and scratched Artemis's ears, her fingers tangling with his as she replied, "I thought you'd never ask."

* * * *

Also from 1001 Dark Nights and Darynda Jones, discover The Graveyard Shift and The Gravedigger's Son.

Sign up for the 1001 Dark Nights Newsletter
and be entered to win a Tiffany Key necklace.

There's a contest every month!

Go to www.1001DarkNights.com to subscribe.

**As a bonus, all subscribers can download
FIVE FREE exclusive books!**

Discover 1001 Dark Nights Collection Nine

DRAGON UNBOUND by Donna Grant
A Dragon Kings Novella

NOTHING BUT INK by Carrie Ann Ryan
A Montgomery Ink: Fort Collins Novella

THE MASTERMIND by Dylan Allen
A Rivers Wilde Novella

JUST ONE WISH by Carly Phillips
A Kingston Family Novella

BEHIND CLOSED DOORS by Skye Warren
A Rochester Novella

GOSSAMER IN THE DARKNESS by Kristen Ashley
A Fantasyland Novella

DELIGHTED by Lexi Blake
A Masters and Mercenaries Novella

THE GRAVESIDE BAR AND GRILL by Darynda Jones
A Charley Davidson Novella

THE ANTI-FAN AND THE IDOL by Rachel Van Dyken
A My Summer In Seoul Novella

CHARMED BY YOU by J. Kenner
A Stark Security Novella

THE CLOSE-UP by Kennedy Ryan
A Hollywood Renaissance Novella

DESCEND TO DARKNESS by Heather Graham
A Krewe of Hunters Novella

BOND OF PASSION by Larissa Ione
A Demonica Novella

JUST WHAT I NEEDED by Kylie Scott
A Stage Dive Novella

THE SCRAMBLE by Kristen Proby
A Single in Seattle Novella

Also from Blue Box Press

THE BAIT by C.W. Gortner and M.J. Rose

THE FASHION ORPHANS by Randy Susan Meyers and M.J. Rose

TAKING THE LEAP by Kristen Ashley
A River Rain Novel

SAPPHIRE SUNSET by Christopher Rice writing as C. Travis Rice
A Sapphire Cove Novel

THE WAR OF TWO QUEENS by Jennifer L. Armentrout
A Blood and Ash Novel

THE MURDERS AT FLEAT HOUSE by Lucinda Riley

THE HEIST by C.W. Gortner and M.J. Rose

SAPPHIRE SPRING by Christopher Rice writing as C. Travis Rice
A Sapphire Cove Novel

MAKING THE MATCH by Kristen Ashley
A River Rain Novel

A LIGHT IN THE FLAME by Jennifer L. Armentrout
A Flesh and Fire Novel

Discover More Darynda Jones

The Graveyard Shift: A Charley Davidson Novella

Guarding a precocious five-year-old who is half-human, half-god, and 100% destined to save the world is no easy feat.

Garrett Swopes was the ultimate skeptic until he met a certain hellion and her husband. They vanished after stopping a catastrophic event and left him, a mere mortal, in charge of protecting their gift to mankind. But when she disappears as well, he needs the help of another breed of hellion. One who can see past the veil of space and time. One who betrayed him.

She will get a truce in the deal, but she will never earn his forgiveness.

Marika Dubois's son—a warrior in the coming war between heaven and hell—was foreseen long before his birth. But to create a child strong enough to endure the trials that lay ahead, she needed a descendant of powerful magics. She found that in Garrett Swopes and tricked him into fathering her son. A ploy he has never forgiven her for. But when he knocks on her door asking for her help, she sees the fierce attraction he tries to deny rise within him.

And Marika has to decide if she dares risk her heart a second time to help the only man she's ever loved.

* * * *

The Gravedigger's Son: A Charley Davidson Novella

The job should have been easy.

Get in. Assess the situation. Get out. But for veteran tracker Quentin Rutherford, things get sticky when the girl he's loved since puberty shows up, conducting her own investigation into the strange occurrences of the small, New Mexico town. He knew it would be a risk coming back to the area, but he had no idea Amber Kowalski had become a bona fide PI, investigating things that go bump in the night. He shouldn't be surprised, however. She can see through the dead as clearly as he can. The real question is, can she see through him?

But is anything that's worth it ever easy?

To say that Amber is shocked to see her childhood crush would be the understatement of her fragile second life. One look at him tells her everything she needs to know. He's changed. So drastically she barely recognizes him. He is savage now, a hardened—in all the right places—demon hunter, and she is simply the awkward, lovestruck girl he left behind.

But she doesn't have time to dwell on the past. A supernatural entity has set up shop, and it's up to them to stop it before it kills again.

While thousands of questions burn inside her, she has to put her concern over him, over what he's become, aside for now. Because he's about to learn one, undeniable fact: she's changed, too.

Betwixt: A Paranormal Women's Fiction Novel

Betwixt & Between, Book One
By Darynda Jones

A Paranormal Women's Fiction with a bit of class, and a lot of sass, for anyone who feels like age is just a number!

Divorced, desperate, and destitute, former restaurateur Defiance Dayne finds out she has been bequeathed a house by a complete stranger. She is surprised, to say the least, and her curiosity gets the better of her. She leaves her beloved Phoenix and heads to one of the most infamous towns in America: Salem, Massachusetts.

She's only there to find out why a woman she's never met would leave her a house. A veritable castle that has seen better days. She couldn't possibly accept it, but the lawyer assigned to the case practically begs her to take it off her hands, mostly because she's scared of it. The house. The inanimate structure that, as far as Dephne can tell, has never hurt a fly.

Though it does come with some baggage. A pesky neighbor who wants her gone. A scruffy cat who's a bit of a jerk. And a handyman bathed in ink who could moonlight as a supermodel for GQ.

She decides to give it three days, and not because of the model. She feels at home in Salem. Safe. But even that comes to a screeching halt when people begin knocking on her door day and night, begging for her help to locate their lost objects.

Come to find out, they think she's a witch. And after a few mysterious mishaps, Dephne is beginning to wonder if they're right.

* * * *

There are two kinds of people in the world:
those who believe in magic and those who are wrong.

I pulled to a stop in front of a sprawling mansion, checked the address the lawyer gave me, then glanced at the mansion again, even more confused than I'd been when I first got the call. No way was this legit. I looked at the numbers on the massive white columns and compared them to the numbers I'd scribbled on a hot pink sticky note. Perfect match. It was one thing for a complete stranger to bequeath me a house. It was quite another for that house to look like a red brick version of Tara from *Gone with the Wind*.

I turned my head to look at the street sign one more time, making sure it said Chestnut, before checking the address a third time. Still a perfect match. Maybe I heard it wrong. Or wrote it down wrong. Or I'd entered the *Twilight Zone*. As I sat steeping in a light marinade of seasonal herbs and bewilderment, weighing my options—medication, electroshock therapy, exorcism—an urgent knock sounded on the window of my vintage mint green Volkswagen Beetle, a.k.a., the bug. I jumped in response, the movement quite possibly dislocating a rib.

A feminine voice shrieked at me as though the barrier between us was a concrete wall instead of a piece of glass. "Ms. Dayne?"

I put an arm around my ribcage to protect it from any further damage and turned to the panic-stricken woman enveloped from head to toe in neon purple.

"Hi!" she shouted.

Seriously, every article of clothing she wore—beret, scarf, wool coat, knitted mittens—were all a shade of purple so bright my pupils had to adjust.

"Are you Ms. Dayne?"

And I liked purple. Really, I did. Just not a shade so bright it made my eyes water. Not unlike pepper spray. Or napalm.

I cracked the window and gave a cautious, "Mrs. Richter?"

The woman shoved her mitted hand into the narrow opening I'd created. "So nice to meet you. What do you think?"

I took her hand a microsecond before she snatched it back and stepped to the side to allow me to exit.

Mrs. Richter, a woman only a couple of years older than my own forty-four years of hard labor with little reward, hurried to the hood of the bug and pulled a stack of papers from a manila envelope. A stack of papers that probably needed my signature.

A needlelike cramp tightened the muscles in my stomach. This was all happening too fast. Much like my life of late.

After the first wave of pain subsided—the same pain I'd been having for months now—I pushed a wind-blown lock of black hair over my ear and followed her.

"Mrs. Richter, I don't understand any of this. Why would someone I don't know leave me a house? Especially one that looks straight out of Architectural Digest."

"What?" She glanced up from her task of wrangling the paperwork in the icy wind and let her gaze bounce from the house to me then back to the house. "Oh, heavens. I'm so sorry. Mrs. Goode didn't leave you *this* house. I just wanted to meet here because her house is, well—" She cleared her throat and tried to tame a strand of blond hair that whipped across her forehead. "It's persnickety."

Relief flooded every cell in my body. Either that or the Adderall I'd had in lieu of breakfast was finally kicking in. Still, how in the Sam Spade could a house be persnickety?

Deciding that was a question for another day, I released a breath I didn't know I'd been holding. "That's actually a bit of a weight off my shoulders. There's no way I could afford the taxes and insurance on this place, much less the upkeep."

"Oh, well, that shouldn't be a problem. Somehow the taxes on Percival are stuck in the fifties. Cheapest on the block, but you didn't hear that from me. Also, there's the money that Mrs. Goode—"

"Percival?"

She leaned into the bone-chilling breeze, and whispered, "The house."

About Darynda Jones

NY Times and *USA Today* Bestselling Author Darynda Jones has won numerous awards for her work and her books have been translated into 17 languages. As a born storyteller, Darynda grew up spinning tales of dashing damsels and heroes in distress for any unfortunate soul who happened by, certain they went away the better for it. She penned the internationally bestselling Charley Davidson series and is currently working on several beloved projects, most notably the Sunshine Vicram Mystery Series with St. Martin's Press and the Betwixt and Between Series of paranormal women's fiction. She lives in the Land of Enchantment, also known as New Mexico, with her husband and two beautiful sons, the Mighty, Mighty Jones Boys.

She can be found at http://www.daryndajones.com

Discover 1001 Dark Nights

COLLECTION ONE
FOREVER WICKED by Shayla Black ~ CRIMSON TWILIGHT by Heather Graham ~ CAPTURED IN SURRENDER by Liliana Hart ~ SILENT BITE: A SCANGUARDS WEDDING by Tina Folsom ~ DUNGEON GAMES by Lexi Blake ~ AZAGOTH by Larissa Ione ~ NEED YOU NOW by Lisa Renee Jones ~ SHOW ME, BABY by Cherise Sinclair~ ROPED IN by Lorelei James ~ TEMPTED BY MIDNIGHT by Lara Adrian ~ THE FLAME by Christopher Rice ~ CARESS OF DARKNESS by Julie Kenner

COLLECTION TWO
WICKED WOLF by Carrie Ann Ryan ~ WHEN IRISH EYES ARE HAUNTING by Heather Graham ~ EASY WITH YOU by Kristen Proby ~ MASTER OF FREEDOM by Cherise Sinclair ~ CARESS OF PLEASURE by Julie Kenner ~ ADORED by Lexi Blake ~ HADES by Larissa Ione ~ RAVAGED by Elisabeth Naughton ~ DREAM OF YOU by Jennifer L. Armentrout ~ STRIPPED DOWN by Lorelei James ~ RAGE/KILLIAN by Alexandra Ivy/Laura Wright ~ DRAGON KING by Donna Grant ~ PURE WICKED by Shayla Black ~ HARD AS STEEL by Laura Kaye ~ STROKE OF MIDNIGHT by Lara Adrian ~ ALL HALLOWS EVE by Heather Graham ~ KISS THE FLAME by Christopher Rice~ DARING HER LOVE by Melissa Foster ~ TEASED by Rebecca Zanetti ~ THE PROMISE OF SURRENDER by Liliana Hart

COLLECTION THREE
HIDDEN INK by Carrie Ann Ryan ~ BLOOD ON THE BAYOU by Heather Graham ~ SEARCHING FOR MINE by Jennifer Probst ~ DANCE OF DESIRE by Christopher Rice ~ ROUGH RHYTHM by Tessa Bailey ~ DEVOTED by Lexi Blake ~ Z by Larissa Ione ~ FALLING UNDER YOU by Laurelin Paige ~ EASY FOR KEEPS by Kristen Proby ~ UNCHAINED by Elisabeth Naughton ~ HARD TO SERVE by Laura Kaye ~ DRAGON FEVER by Donna Grant ~ KAYDEN/SIMON by Alexandra Ivy/Laura Wright ~ STRUNG UP by Lorelei James ~ MIDNIGHT UNTAMED by Lara Adrian ~

TRICKED by Rebecca Zanetti ~ DIRTY WICKED by Shayla Black ~ THE ONLY ONE by Lauren Blakely ~ SWEET SURRENDER by Liliana Hart

COLLECTION FOUR
ROCK CHICK REAWAKENING by Kristen Ashley ~ ADORING INK by Carrie Ann Ryan ~ SWEET RIVALRY by K. Bromberg ~ SHADE'S LADY by Joanna Wylde ~ RAZR by Larissa Ione ~ ARRANGED by Lexi Blake ~ TANGLED by Rebecca Zanetti ~ HOLD ME by J. Kenner ~ SOMEHOW, SOME WAY by Jennifer Probst ~ TOO CLOSE TO CALL by Tessa Bailey ~ HUNTED by Elisabeth Naughton ~ EYES ON YOU by Laura Kaye ~ BLADE by Alexandra Ivy/Laura Wright ~ DRAGON BURN by Donna Grant ~ TRIPPED OUT by Lorelei James ~ STUD FINDER by Lauren Blakely ~ MIDNIGHT UNLEASHED by Lara Adrian ~ HALLOW BE THE HAUNT by Heather Graham ~ DIRTY FILTHY FIX by Laurelin Paige ~ THE BED MATE by Kendall Ryan ~ NIGHT GAMES by CD Reiss ~ NO RESERVATIONS by Kristen Proby ~ DAWN OF SURRENDER by Liliana Hart

COLLECTION FIVE
BLAZE ERUPTING by Rebecca Zanetti ~ ROUGH RIDE by Kristen Ashley ~ HAWKYN by Larissa Ione ~ RIDE DIRTY by Laura Kaye ~ ROME'S CHANCE by Joanna Wylde ~ THE MARRIAGE ARRANGEMENT by Jennifer Probst ~ SURRENDER by Elisabeth Naughton ~ INKED NIGHTS by Carrie Ann Ryan ~ ENVY by Rachel Van Dyken ~ PROTECTED by Lexi Blake ~ THE PRINCE by Jennifer L. Armentrout ~ PLEASE ME by J. Kenner ~ WOUND TIGHT by Lorelei James ~ STRONG by Kylie Scott ~ DRAGON NIGHT by Donna Grant ~ TEMPTING BROOKE by Kristen Proby ~ HAUNTED BE THE HOLIDAYS by Heather Graham ~ CONTROL by K. Bromberg ~ HUNKY HEARTBREAKER by Kendall Ryan ~ THE DARKEST CAPTIVE by Gena Showalter

COLLECTION SIX
DRAGON CLAIMED by Donna Grant ~ ASHES TO INK by Carrie Ann Ryan ~ ENSNARED by Elisabeth Naughton ~ EVERMORE by Corinne Michaels ~ VENGEANCE by Rebecca Zanetti ~ ELI'S TRIUMPH by Joanna Wylde ~ CIPHER by Larissa Ione ~

RESCUING MACIE by Susan Stoker ~ ENCHANTED by Lexi Blake ~ TAKE THE BRIDE by Carly Phillips ~ INDULGE ME by J. Kenner ~ THE KING by Jennifer L. Armentrout ~ QUIET MAN by Kristen Ashley ~ ABANDON by Rachel Van Dyken ~ THE OPEN DOOR by Laurelin Paige~ CLOSER by Kylie Scott ~ SOMETHING JUST LIKE THIS by Jennifer Probst ~ BLOOD NIGHT by Heather Graham ~ TWIST OF FATE by Jill Shalvis ~ MORE THAN PLEASURE YOU by Shayla Black ~ WONDER WITH ME by Kristen Proby ~ THE DARKEST ASSASSIN by Gena Showalter

COLLECTION EIGHT

DRAGON REVEALED by Donna Grant ~ CAPTURED IN INK by Carrie Ann Ryan ~ SECURING JANE by Susan Stoker ~ WILD WIND by Kristen Ashley ~ DARE TO TEASE by Carly Phillips ~ VAMPIRE by Rebecca Zanetti ~ MAFIA KING by Rachel Van Dyken ~ THE GRAVEDIGGER'S SON by Darynda Jones ~ FINALE by Skye Warren ~ MEMORIES OF YOU by J. Kenner ~ SLAYED BY DARKNESS by Alexandra Ivy ~ TREASURED by Lexi Blake ~ THE DAREDEVIL by Dylan Allen ~ BOND OF DESTINY by Larissa Ione ~ MORE THAN POSSESS YOU by Shayla Black ~ HAUNTED HOUSE by Heather Graham ~ MAN FOR ME by Laurelin Paige ~ THE RHYTHM METHOD by Kylie Scott ~ JONAH BENNETT by Tijan ~ CHANGE WITH ME by Kristen Proby ~ THE DARKEST DESTINY by Gena Showalter

Discover Blue Box Press

TAME ME by J. Kenner ~ TEMPT ME by J. Kenner ~ DAMIEN by J. Kenner ~ TEASE ME by J. Kenner ~ REAPER by Larissa Ione ~ THE SURRENDER GATE by Christopher Rice ~ SERVICING THE TARGET by Cherise Sinclair ~ THE LAKE OF LEARNING by Steve Berry and M.J. Rose ~ THE MUSEUM OF MYSTERIES by Steve Berry and M.J. Rose ~ TEASE ME by J. Kenner ~ FROM BLOOD AND ASH by Jennifer L. Armentrout ~ QUEEN MOVE by Kennedy Ryan ~ THE HOUSE OF LONG AGO by Steve Berry and M.J. Rose ~ THE BUTTERFLY ROOM by Lucinda Riley ~ A KINGDOM OF FLESH AND FIRE by Jennifer L. Armentrout ~ THE LAST TIARA by M.J. Rose ~ THE CROWN OF GILDED BONES by Jennifer L. Armentrout ~ THE MISSING SISTER by Lucinda Riley ~ THE END

OF FOREVER by Steve Berry and M.J. Rose ~ THE STEAL by C. W. Gortner and M.J. Rose ~ CHASING SERENITY by Kristen Ashley ~ A SHADOW IN THE EMBER by Jennifer L. Armentrout

On Behalf of 1001 Dark Nights,

Liz Berry, M.J. Rose, and Jillian Stein would like to thank ~

Steve Berry
Doug Scofield
Benjamin Stein
Kim Guidroz
Social Butterfly PR
Asha Hossain
Chris Graham
Chelle Olson
Kasi Alexander
Jessica Saunders
Dylan Stockton
Kate Boggs
Richard Blake
and Simon Lipskar

Made in United States
Orlando, FL
24 August 2022

21474330R00064